"Run program Male Alcaini One," she commanded.

Ez'iri's voice greeted her. "Rayne'iri, I have programmed what you requested. This unit is small, well-used, and will not be missed for a few hours. However, the technology is aged. The program is not sophisticated, but should meet your—needs." Ez'iri's voice trilled with amusement. "I have programmed the unit to adjust according to your physiology, but you must still use caution. The power cell will last one quarter of an hour. Take your pleasure, my friend."

The unit began to glow with a soft, silvery light, as if captured starlight lurked somewhere in the box. From the port, a pale, amorphous blob of plasma emerged, shooting up about six feet and gradually coalescing into a humanoid shape. Her eyes dropped to what hung between his legs.

The pit of her stomach fluttered and a blush heated her cheeks, spreading down her neck to the tops of her breasts beneath the lab coat she'd hastily thrown on to retrieve her package.

Not one, but two cocks hung, heavy and somnolent. Sleeping beasts born in the sky, to assuage an earthy, yet unearthly hunger.

Finally, after an eternity, he was solid.

Wordlessly, he came to her. The "passing resemblance" to Ez'iri's kinsman was the understatement of the century.

"Come here, secret fantasy lover," she said, feeling free to indulge in a little over-emotive dialogue, away from prying eyes. "There's no one around to watch our little secret."

Alien Communion

Xandra Gregory

Liquid Silver Books
Indianapolis, Indiana

Published By:
Liquid Silver Books
10509 Sedgegrass Dr.
Indianapolis, IN 46235

Liquid Silver Books publishes books online and in trade paperback. Visit our site at
http://www.liquidsilverbooks.com

Manufactured in the United States of America

ISBN Ten: 1-59578-241-9
ISBN Thirteen: 978-1-59578-241-0

Cover: Will Kramer

Dedication

To the wonderful Mr. Xandra, who's believed in me forever, and to my incomparable critique partner Roxy Harte, because no matter what other craziness lands on us, we'll always have the writing.

Alien Communion

Chapter One

"In conclusion, because of the valuable work to be done in the field of sexual psychology, the Foundation is pleased to welcome Dr. Kenneth Taggart to the research staff."

A light smattering of applause greeted the announcement. Rayne Warren stared intently at her notepad, her entire consciousness focused on keeping a humiliated blush from staining her cheeks. Every other member of the small group rose to welcome their new team member. Of all the people in the world, why did it have to be Ken?

The eleven people assembled in the room were just about the only people in the entire world who knew of the existence of the Alcaini, an advanced race of aliens that initiated tentative contact with humans a few short months ago. Not counting a scant handful at the Foundation's highest level with ties to the government, her ex-boyfriend now rounded the troupe out to an even dozen.

It took a few minutes to register that everyone was staring at her. She blinked, emerging from inside her head. Kenneth stood before her expectantly, waiting to be acknowledged. The small, supremely confident smile on his face aped the one he'd worn the time when their relationship had suddenly changed from lovers to observer and subject. It made her skin crawl.

She forced the remembered hurt away and said, "Welcome aboard, Dr. Taggart." No hint of emotion gave her away.

"*Dr.* Warren," he said. The once-over he gave her was frank and condescending at the same time. The inflection on her title could have been imaginary, but she doubted it. "I'm honored to have been asked to fill the, ah, holes of your research."

The looks of her teammates turned speculative as she lost the battle with her blush. Filling holes, indeed! She smiled sweetly at him. "I'm sure you'll have no problems filling the holes in my *research*."

Someone snickered. Buhlmeier, a linguist, said, "Hey, we all know Warren's got the smallest holes to fill."

Reese poked him. "And your mama's got the biggest." The anthro-specialist's comeback invoked a ripple of laughter from the group.

"Bite me."

"Okay, people, enough with the mama jokes and sexual innuendo," Peter Cerznyk, the de facto leader of the team, held up his hand.

Buhlmeier snorted. Rayne couldn't help smiling at the obviously juvenile turn the group gestalt had taken. Better that than focusing on her humiliating past with the newest team member.

Cerznyk passed out the day's assignments. To her dismay, she found herself paired with Taggart, viewing study vids the Alcaini had provided in the initial information exchange. She grimaced. Probably the equivalent of hygiene films, complete with watery-sounding music and a cheesy announcer.

She left as soon as Cerznyk finished the list, pushing open the swinging doors of the break room for some caffeinated composure.

Taggart followed her. "Rayne."

She turned. "What is it, Kenneth?" She injected as much annoyance into her voice as she could muster.

He frowned. "I would have thought you'd have moved past the circumstances of our last meeting. Isn't it past time you accepted the help in the spirit it was given?"

"Help? Is that what you deluded yourself into thinking you were doing?" She pulled her cup from the little dishwasher and set it on the counter with more force than a poor cup deserved. "And what, exactly, was the spirit in which it was given, besides the advancement of your career?" She splashed coffee into the cup. Dark rivulets ran down the outside, temporarily marring the 'Support bacteria—it's the only culture some people have' message.

There was no shame quite like the shame of having to read the intimate details of her sexual encounters in a research paper entitled 'Repression of sexuality in response to advancement of intellect in the feminine psyche.'

She added cream and sugar, haphazardly dumping the powders from their canisters. Her stirring was more suited to separating plasma from blood than blending morning beverage.

"Rayne, you know that paper was only a by-product of our relationship."

"Children are the by-products of relationships, Kenneth. Community property is the by-product of relationships. Research papers are not." She pushed past him and out into the hallway.

She had no idea how she was going to sit in a media room with him for hours and watch biology vids. She hoped they would be interesting enough for her to forget he was there.

He followed her down the hall. "Come on, Rayne. Let's put that behind us. No one knows the identity of the subject of that study. Your secret is safe with me."

She paused long enough to glare at him. "Listen carefully, Doctor Taggart. I will work with you on this team for as long as I have to. But don't expect me to ever forget about it." She pulled open the door to the media room and went inside, not bothering with the lights.

"You would have done the same thing," he said sullenly.

"I wouldn't have betrayed the trust of someone I loved just for the sake of a research paper."

"If you hadn't been so damn difficult to please…"

She rounded on him. "You will *not* pin this on me! *You* were the one who kept notes about our sex life and made the decision to publish every dirty little secret I had."

"Look, I just wanted to help. There had to be a reason you were never satisfied. I knew if I looked at your psyche, it would tell me why, and maybe help you solve your problem. Can I help it if the subject is of interest to so many people that it was my duty as a scientist to publish it?"

She made a disgusted sound. "Oh, save it for someone stupid enough to believe it. I'm sick of listening to your excuses."

"Rayne, I know you were hurt and I really am sorry," he said calmly. "I hope that some day you can understand how many people that paper helped."

She busied herself with rigging up the AV equipment, not trusting herself to speak. Nothing could gall her more than to admit he was right, and he was. That paper opened doors that even hardcore feminists couldn't find fault with.

Yet it didn't do a damn thing for her. The yearning for something more never went away. The knowledge that something had to be out there to complete her remained as frustratingly present as it had ever been.

The video screen flickered to life. Kenneth said, "Let yourself heal from the experience. If you don't, you'll never be able to fully contribute to this research project."

"I'm doing plenty," she said tightly, occupying herself with the DVD controller.

"Not according to our superiors," he said. "I was brought on board because you can't seem to offer anything more than a mechanical analysis of Alcaini mating practices."

The crimson blush hit her, hot and suddenly. "I've been working with precious little data," she said defensively.

"There's a wealth of data in other areas that can be analyzed and extrapolated. If you have the right way of looking at it."

She flopped into a chair and folded her arms as the DVD began broadcasting. "Let's just look at the new information and drop it."

He sat in the chair across from her. She thanked the powers that be for the solid conference table between them. She stared at the empty blue screen, waiting for something to appear and take her mind away from the edge of the huge black pit of despair that threatened to swallow her whole.

Emptiness seemed to be the one theme in her life— her constant companion. No matter what—or who—she did, something always lacked. A single missing piece in a zillion-piece puzzle that left a hole no bigger than a molecule, but whose presence brought that piece's absence to glaring attention.

This project brought her as close to fulfillment as she'd ever dreamed. After Kenneth and the humiliation she suffered at his hands, she abandoned all hope for her private life and sought completion through her work. The Alcaini people, and the top-secret information exchange between Alcaini and humans, absorbed her ever since she'd learned—abruptly and firsthand—of their existence.

An Alcaini female appeared on the screen. She began speaking in the melodic modality of the Alcaini common language. English subtitles appeared on the screen. "This communication is designed to answer queries on Alcaini reproductive functions. Elsewhere in the program is a comprehensive medical encyclopedia related to the subject."

"Do you suppose they have a series of these from us?" he asked.

Apparently, Dr. Taggart wasn't entirely up to speed on the project's history. "They made their own prior to initial contact."

He put two and two together quickly. "No shit," he murmured. "Alien abductees?"

She nodded, keeping her lips tightly closed. The way he said it reminded her that she kept company with some of the most colorful elements of the fringe population.

"I guess not all of the fruit loops who claim to have anal probes in UFOs are lying out their probed asses."

She offered him a weak smile. "I was one of their abductees." She stared straight at the screen. True to her initial hunch, the vid was looking like an updated version of a hygiene film. A 3D rendering of male and female internal sex organs slowly revolved, portions glowing as their names and primary functions appeared on the screen. "And no, they didn't give me an anal probe, so you can kill that joke before it hits air and stinks up the place."

"Good God, Rayne, I had no idea…"

"Apparently, you're not the only one who thinks I make a good test subject." The internal organs shrunk in perspective and located themselves in two Alcaini outlines that began to coalesce into male and female forms.

"Rayne…"

She shushed him. "Look—it's getting interesting." The male form faded and the female form morphed into an actual female Alcaini. She actually resembled a human quite closely. If not for the color of her skin and the bony ridges along her skull and torso, she wouldn't look any different from Rayne herself, as she stepped naked out of the shower. The Alcaini woman's skin glowed a deep rose, indicating, according to the screen, sexual arousal. How embarrassing, she thought. At least if she had one of those stray, 'wonder what he looks like naked' thoughts, it wouldn't be plastered all over her skin for the world to see.

Then again, the Alcaini had a very matter-of-fact view about sex. Reese's anthropological analysis had likened it to how most humans viewed eating. Apparently their culture hadn't ever hit the point where mating turned taboo.

It's the taboo that gives us such hang-ups, she thought. Lord knew she was the poster child for taboos and hang-ups. But even Kenneth with his award-winning, extensive psychological analysis of her attitude couldn't un-hang her into contentment.

The male Alcaini coalesced as the female faded from the screen. As his form took shape, she noted one very distinct difference between male Alcaini and male humans. She couldn't keep herself from gasping out a startled, "Oh, my!"

Across the table, Kenneth shifted uncomfortably. "There's a sight that ought to make a man feel inadequate," he joked lamely.

Indeed, she thought. *And a woman wet and weak-kneed.* "You'll get used to seeing the differences in physiology," she said, surprised that her voice sounded so normal. As the form continued to take on more realistic features, she became aware of her heart beating faster inside her chest. A low pulling in her abdomen, pulsating with her accelerated heartbeat, made her shift in her chair. As she crossed and uncrossed her legs, she realized that the backs of her thighs were damp from a sudden sweat.

All over a computer-generated 3D rendering of an alien. Ridiculous!

The Alcaini female joined the male, and the two figures moved into copulating position, affording them a close-up glance at the female anatomy that matched the unique male anatomy.

"I stand corrected," Kenneth murmured. "I think the sight of her is definitely more inclined to make a man feel inadequate."

She laughed, a tight, not-quite-comfortable sound. The two figures on the screen turned semi-transparent to demonstrate just exactly how the parts all fit together. "This is, without a doubt, the weirdest porno I've ever seen."

He laughed, dissolving some of the tension. The figures moved faster, simulating the entire act of copulation. It looked like Alcaini mating practices leaned towards the rough stuff. Yet as she watched, her clinical detachment slipped further and further away as the irresistible urges of imagination came to the fore.

Her mouth went dry. Her tongue darted out to moisten suddenly parched lips. A frisson of awareness burned a path from her chest to her groin, sending tingles out to her extremities and back again. Heat swelled from her abdomen and she grew startlingly aware of the tight press of fabric against her skin.

The thought was too bizarre to even acknowledge. But it settled into her mind, and with it, the yearning emptiness within her reared its head, as if it sensed something that could silence it nearby.

An Alcaini lover…

But all she had to do was look at Kenneth to keep the thought firmly in the realms of 'not bloody likely.' In fact, no one on the planet—scratch that, no being in the universe—would ever have the chance to betray her secret desires again.

The thought, while relegated to the extreme outer edges of her conscious mind, refused to disappear completely. After the video completed, she forced herself into her most clinical, professional behavior.

Kenneth tried to pull her out of it. While she used terms like 'reproductive behaviors,' he insisted that they were 'lovemaking techniques.' The aggravating tendency did nothing for her concentration. The third time she quibbled with him about terminology, he flung a pen across the table in frustration. "Dammit, Rayne, will you cease being so bloody squeamish already?"

She bristled. "I'm not being squeamish, I'm being scientific. Objective. I'm not painting up the biology with fluffy romantic colors."

He shot her a humorless smile. "No, you're certainly not. Your observations are as flat as line drawings. They capture no essence, no insight into the Alcaini."

"Fine, we'll use your language to present the day's work to the team. And we'll see just how much scientific value they find in purple prose and euphemisms."

"Pay attention, Rayne," he said tightly. "You might learn something."

* ~ *

Later, when they reconvened with the research team, she approached things a little more calmly. The DVD no longer played in the background, haunting her subconscious with erotic possibilities that didn't exist in the real world.

Kenneth invited her to present the overview of the basics of Alcaini reproduction. She took it as the truce it was meant to be. She knew, and he would, too, that personality conflicts were insignificant in the face of the vastly more important and groundbreaking research they were doing. If they didn't at least try to get along, they could both find themselves out on their asses.

She focused on the group. "Alcaini bear remarkable resemblances to humans. But they also have marked differences. We're both bipedal humanoid, but our reproductive systems and theirs have some, uh, significant differences." She went on to describe the most significant differences in reproduction and sex, then opened the table for questions.

Reese spoke up. "I noted in my anthro research that taboos on sexuality don't seem to exist in the Alcaini culture. Can you theorize if there's a biological reason for that?"

She nodded. "The skin tone of Alcaini people changes with their emotions, including sexual arousal. It's as obvious a display as an erection on a naked man." As soon as she spoke the analogy, she regretted it. Why, oh why did she say that with Buhlmeier in the room?

True to form, he pounced on it. "Like your skin tone's changing now?"

Being a natural carrot-top, she might as well be Alcaini. Her blushes could light up a dark room. She flipped him off. "Actually, worse. I only blush. The Alcaini's entire body changes color. Closer to what a chameleon would do."

"As opposed to an uptight redhead?" Buhlmeier cracked.

She threw a pencil at him.

Cerznyk held up a hand. "Enough, people. Rayne, can you answer the question at the top of the list in the mind of the common man?"

She looked at him confusedly. "What question would that be?" She, herself, would have a million of them. She still did. No particular one stood out in her mind.

"Can humans mate with Alcaini?"

"Ah. Um. No. At least, not without help. Alcaini genetics are more complex than ours are. So any half-breeds would have to have assistance from a lab."

At Cerznyk's blank look, Kenneth interjected. "I think he means, are sexual relations even possible? The answer to that is yes, there are tab A's that fit into slot B's in both our species."

That thought came screaming back into her consciousness. She put both her hands on the table in front of her to stop their sudden trembling. Good thing she was already blushing, otherwise her face would have given her away in a heartbeat.

Kenneth continued. "The question is, though, would it be wise or safe to try it? At this point, perhaps a visual reminder of the, uh, differences in our bodies would go a long way towards underscoring the issues rising from it."

She took that as her cue and hit the DVD controller. The Alcaini nudes appeared, in all their slowly-revolving splendor. Buhlmeier emitted a low whistle.

Kenneth took over the presentation then, enthusing on the elegance of the Alcaini 'lovemaking techniques' in relation to their mental states. Rayne dismissed it as a bunch of nonsense, but as she looked around at her coworkers, she realized she was the only one who thought so. Even Buhlmeier listened with rapt attention as Kenneth painted a picture of a culture with hedonistically decadent mating practices.

Finally, she had to say something. "Excuse me, Kenneth, but how can you infer such a detailed profile about the Alcaini, based on what amounted to junior high health class footage?"

His smile was condescending. "This is my specialty, Rayne." The unspoken, "you of all people should know that" hung in the air, palpable enough for even Buhlmeier's ears to perk up.

She glared at him, then at Kenneth. "I think you're making some pretty wild assumptions."

"Not at all." His tone encompassed the entire room. He looked past her to Cerznyk. "By observing elements like posture, vocal inflections, eye contact, and other non-verbal body cues, I've drawn a solid conclusion based on a significant amount of evidence. Couple that with Dr. Warren's clinical biological information, and the sexual psyche of the Alcaini becomes a known entity."

Rayne fought the urge to roll her eyes. When would Cerznyk and the rest of them see through Kenneth's double-talk? Cerznyk put up an inquiring pencil. Good, she thought. Ask questions, poke holes in his overblown ego.

Fifteen minutes later, as they filed out of the room for the day, Cerznyk put a hand on her arm. "Just a minute, Rayne."

Her stomach bottomed out. Kenneth's ego—and his theories—had withstood the team's questions altogether too well.

Cerznyk's eyes weren't unkind, behind his wire-framed glasses. "Rayne, your contribution to the project has been very valuable so far." He waited.

"Um, thanks." This wasn't good. If anything, she knew the tricks on how to take someone down a notch. First catch them off guard with a compliment. She waited for the heavier shoe to drop.

Cerznyk sighed. "Kenneth made some very effective connections today that I want you to think about. I'm aware that the two of you have a personal history…"

"Ancient history," she said firmly. "It has no bearing on our work."

"Right. Then you should have no trouble allowing him to mentor you."

She blinked. "Excuse me? Don't you mean for me to mentor him?" Besides Cerznyk, she was the most senior member of the team.

He looked down at his neat, manicured fingernails. "No, I mean for him to mentor you. Dr. Taggart made intuitive and insightful conclusions based on the material presented. While your clinical analysis was helpful, it was…flat. One-dimensional."

She pulled back. He might as well have slapped her, for all he tried to soften the blow. "But my work is based on sound empirical data."

"Sometimes that just isn't enough," he said. "We need to wring every possible observation out of this data in order to understand the Alcaini. This is an historic time for humanity. If we fail to understand some nuance of the Alcaini, we could create an incident of galactic proportions." He paused, as if to let her absorb the full extent of his words. "The Alcaini have requested another meeting, and specifically requested your presence. I want to send Dr. Taggart along with you."

"But he's never met them," she protested. "In fact, he didn't even know until today that they had previous test subjects."

"Then it's up to you to make sure he has adequate foreknowledge. If you give yourself a little time to get over the professional pride, you'll see the wisdom in letting Dr. Taggart help extend your skills." Cerznyk rose then, indicating the interview was over.

Rayne sat alone in the room, fighting a furious blush and the urge to cry. Damn Kenneth and his insights, and damn Cerznyk for thinking they were so great.

Damn Kenneth was waiting for her when she left the room. "Rayne."

"I don't want to talk to you right now," she said tightly, afraid she would lose it.

"I know what Cerznyk said." He followed her as she stalked down the hall. "It's not an insult." He put his hand on her arm.

She shook him off. "I said I don't want to talk about it."

He handed her a folder.

"What's this?"

"It's my research paper." At her frown, he held up a hand. "Read it. Objectively, with the eye of a scientist."

"I'd rather puke."

"Childish," he chided. "Look, as long as you refuse to acknowledge your repression, Cerznyk and every other boss you have will always find something lacking in your work."

With that last barb, he let her go. Impotent fury seethed in her. How dare he! Something lacking, indeed! The thoughts traveled round and round in her head, late into the night.

Lacking...

Missing...

Yearning...

Chapter Two

She had to come to terms with the fact that Cerznyk wouldn't let her see the Alcaini again without Kenneth, but she didn't have to like it. Instead, she tried on her own to emulate Kenneth. In the privacy of her bedroom, she studied the hygiene film with single-minded intent.

Without an audience, her fingers kept aiming the rewind button to when the male Alcaini appeared. The image of that naked male never failed to weaken her knees.

Kenneth's words haunted her. *Humans and Alcaini can engage in relations.* She conveniently dropped the latter part of his conclusion—the part about whether or not they should. Her room was dark, she was alone, and no one else was privy to her thoughts.

She returned to the chapter of the DVD that demonstrated the Alcaini couple in coitus. The images sank into her brain as she watched it over and over, trying to see what Kenneth would see, what Cerznyk wanted her to see, what someone not just second best would see.

"It's no use," she said aloud to the darkened room. Her mind was too logical, and while the sight of the coupling turned her on, it was purely an animalistic reaction. She'd get the same thrill out of watching horses mate. In fact, her lids grew heavier each time she watched the footage.

Comfortably relaxed in her bed, she drifted, her mind no longer on the footage on screen. She drew in a deep breath and caught the scent of exotic flowers. Another deep breath and the walls of her room faded away into darkness. The air grew heavy, as did her limbs and suddenly, she was standing, naked, in a cavernous dark room she recognized as the Alcaini medical lab.

A light appeared, dim, from directly above, shedding its soft glow. A form emerged from the thick darkness outside the small circle of light.

An Alcaini male appeared, his skin apple-red. The biologist in her noted his particularly strong head and torso ridges. Thickly muscled arms reached out towards her, grasping her upper arms and pulling her towards him. She started. Never had she been this close to an Alcaini male. When she'd been taken, it had been by females.

She felt sheer power in his grasp. The reality of his presence descended upon her, overwhelming her with sensations. His fingers burned brands into her skin. The scent of him—that faintly floral, exotic musk could make her drunk just by inhaling it. His skin held a cool dryness on the surface, but burning heat within.

He leaned in close. His golden yellow eyes, so alien, bored into hers. His forked tongue flicked out, tasting the air just in front of her lips.

She licked her own lips in response. Her whole body went liquid with desire. Her nipples tightened, aching for contact, and creamy dampness pooled between her legs. The softest, tiniest moan came out of her throat. Her body strained towards his, yet she couldn't physically move. If he would only lean closer!

He took a breath. Her nipples came into contact with the desert heat of his chest.

"Look," he whispered. "See. See as a woman sees."

She woke with a start, heart slamming in her chest. Her t-shirt was soaked with sweat and her whole body flushed a deep crimson. The monitor screen burned a steady blue—the DVD must have finished playing a while ago.

She licked her lips and rose from her bed on unsteady legs, padding into the bathroom for a glass of water to cool her parched throat. She let the water run as she gulped the cool liquid in the glass, then plunged her hands under the faucet and splashed her face.

The Alcaini man had said something—*See as a woman sees*.

She frowned.

She found the DVD chapter with the mating and played it again.

Things were definitely different this time. The figures on the screen still resembled not much more than interestingly engaged polygons, but her mind remembered the vividness of the dream—the real Alcaini man, his scent, his heat.

Suddenly, the polygons became something...more. She could see the power and intricacy in the way his hips swiveled, and the coordinating response in his mate. The coiled strength in his fingers as they caressed her flanks, the fluidity of her movements meeting his.

How would it feel to have a man like that fuck her that way?

Jesus, the mere thought of it brought a rush of liquid heat to her pussy.

Without thought, her fingers moved down to explore the folds of her lower lips. The video shifted focus to zero in on the copulating couple's genitalia, highlighting the exotic difference between Alcaini and human.

Her hips involuntarily thrust upward and her fingers worked faster over her clit. Between the view on screen and the memory of her hot dream of the Alcaini man standing before her, she could indeed see as a woman saw. In the dark, highlighted only by the flickering TV screen, she thrust her fingers deep inside her pussy, moving them in and out in time with the mating couple on the screen. Her hips bucked and the musky scent of her wetness permeated the air.

She thrust another finger into herself, working three fingers in and out, begging herself for more. Her pussy opened to the pulsing of her fingers and the delicious tightening of impending orgasm converged in her lower abdomen.

And yet, something remained absent.

Her eyes focused on the Alcaini, and what made him so uniquely, strangely enticing. One of her fingers moved out of her pussy to circle wetly around her anus, dipping in as she imagined the Alcaini male would. *Two cocks...at the same time...* The mere thought of it sent her hips twisting faster.

She thrust into the air and the shimmering release of orgasm washed over her, drenching her fingers with her own juices, her soft cries echoing in the room. Even as her cunt clenched and clenched again, squeezing her fingers in sensory-rich pulses, it wasn't enough.

The satiation wasn't complete. Her body drifted in post-orgasmic drowse, but something deep inside her core remained untouched, untapped, and unfulfilled. In spite of her physical repletion, an iron shaft of despair lanced through her. She would never be good enough if she couldn't even fulfill her own needs.

* ~ *

The next morning, the folder containing Kenneth's research paper confronted her, centered square in the middle of her kitchen table. Last night had shown her more about herself than about the Alcaini. That empty craving she couldn't put a name to still haunted her. More conscious than ever of her incompleteness, she opened the folder.

It was the act of a desperate woman, to finally want to hear what her ex had to say about her sexual deviances. She spent time on the paper, lingering over the observations and conclusions Kenneth cited that led him to believe she must have traded sexuality for intellect at some point in her development.

She tried to approach it from the mindset that assumed, simply for testing purposes, that he was right. What, then, was she supposed to do to remedy the situation? Get stupid? She could no more let herself abandon her ways of thought than she could pop her actual brain out and leave it in a box while she went out dancing.

* ~ *

She should never have read that stupid research paper, she thought, several hours later on the way to the rendezvous point with the Alcaini. Kenneth's presence next to her only served to undermine her confidence. So she couldn't see things the way he did, make those leaps of faith. But she was excellent at clinical analysis, and if she didn't shake herself out of her funk this minute, she wouldn't be able to offer even that. She'd be a complete failure.

"What are they like, in person?" Kenneth asked softly.

She was surprised to hear insecurity in his voice, although it was perfectly understandable. In a few moments, the human beings who had verifiably met an alien species in person would become an even dozen, with his presence. "They're taller than us. Me. But that's not saying much. You've seen the physical stats. Their skin tone displays their mood, and while we don't have a complete catalogue, we still have enough in common to determine intent and emotion through expressions of face and body, as well as skin. The ridges seem somewhat disconcerting at first," she added, almost as an afterthought. "But they're fascinating, the way they shift beneath the skin." Her tone turned a little dreamy as she thought of her Alcaini dream man's presence.

Kenneth pulled her back to reality. "What was your experience like the first time?"

She took comfort in her somewhat flimsy status as expert. "Like a visit to the doctor's office. They meant to anesthetize me, but for some reason, it didn't take."

His face showed his dawning understanding. "You were First Contact, weren't you? The whole reason the Alcaini chose to contact us in the first place. I'd read that it was a failure of their discretionary systems that instigated contact. But I had no idea it was you."

She remembered the very human startled looks on the faces of the Alcaini med team when she opened her eyes and tried to sit up. Surprise and consternation were apparently not limited to humanity. "They weren't happy that I didn't accommodate them." The image of the long, crystalline staff that one of them pointed at her still gave her a few chills. Who knew if that thing would have vaporized her completely? "They'd been studying us long enough to know some rudimentary communication." The remembered thrill of breakthrough far outshone the fear and unreality of being abducted. "Once they realized I was a scientist— and willing to cooperate—things really started happening."

"Your voice goes soft when you talk about them," Kenneth noted. "Interesting. Do you have affection for them?"

She narrowed her eyes at him. "I don't need you going into shrink mode on me. My experience was unique, historic, and very, very special. I'm not giving you fodder for another research paper."

He tsked in annoyance. "I'm just trying to understand."

They were silent after that. She couldn't help him understand any further. She didn't have the answers herself.

When they reached the rendezvous point, she said, "The Alcaini have some sort of point-to-point matter transference technology. They've set up a station in this warehouse."

"Matter transference? Like in the movies?"

She allowed herself a small smile. "Yeah, only without the special effects. You just sort of, go black for half a second and poof, you're there. Try not to think about it too much, or else you'll get sick." Lord knew she did. The thought of her molecules being ripped apart and sent through an energy beam gave her a world-class case of the willies.

Srivasthani, another member of the team, met them at the entrance of the warehouse. He debriefed Kenneth while Rayne pulled her shirt over her head.

Kenneth started. "What are you doing?"

"Didn't you pay attention? The Transfer station doesn't do clothes."

"You mean—we go naked?"

She smiled cheerfully as she shucked her jeans and underwear. "Yep. You've seen me naked before. Why the fuss?"

He rolled his eyes. "I don't like the idea of meeting an alien species with nothing but my good looks and charm."

"If it helps, they don't go much for clothing, either."

She left him to fumble with his pants and stepped into the tube that served as the transfer station. "Just do it," she said, closing her eyes and holding her breath.

A nauseating moment of disorientation, then nothingness, then panic, then reassuringly firm, solid floor beneath her feet. She opened her eyes to a familiar alien face. "Ez'iri," she said.

The Alcaini woman smiled. "Welcome, Physician Rayne'iri." She appended the Alcaini feminine determinative onto Rayne's name. The Alcaini didn't yet understand the concept of a doctor that wasn't a medical physician, but to Rayne's mind, it was a minor detail. Ez'iri handed her an Alcaini woman's garment. It resembled a filmy kimono. And while it didn't exactly hide much of anything, she was grateful for the illusion.

"It's nice to finally meet you in person," Rayne said.

"The plasma simulation was necessary until we could assure mutual decontamination."

Her first encounter with the Alcaini consisted of the real beings behind an observation window, while some sort of plasma-generated androids actually touched her. She knew they were more than robots, but the technology was sufficiently advanced for her to think they were nothing short of magic.

A moment later, Kenneth joined them. He was sweating and pale as he stumbled out of the transfer station.

Rayne put her arm around him. "I can't promise you'll get used to it, but you'll at least live through it next time."

He offered her a weak smile that froze on his lips at his first glimpse of a real, live alien.

She couldn't blame him. Ez'iri was tall and beautiful. Her ridges stood proudly amidst well-defined bone structure a supermodel would kill for. The fact that she was six feet tall, long-limbed and muscular, added to the overall effect. Golden Alcaini eyes gave the two humans a once-over. "This must be Physician Kenneth'en Taggart."

"Um, yes," he stammered.

"Excellent. I shall have much pleasure in discovering you."

Alarm flashed across Kenneth's face.

Rayne folded her lips between her teeth to keep the laugh from escaping. She'd forgotten the Alcaini speech patterns had such a—sensual tone to them. She handed Kenneth a robe and let him busy himself getting into it.

She glanced around the Alcaini lab. Just as she remembered it, clean lines, elegantly organic in flow. It reminded her of a doctor's office—which it was—but with a noted absence of clinical sterility. Maybe an alternative-health provider's office that doubled as a yoga and meditation center.

Reclining couches lined the walls, each bathed in its own pool of light, just as she remembered it. Recessed shelves and drawers, the lines of which were smooth and sculpted, occupied the space between the medical bays. The round portal that refused to be named something as squarely mundane as a door held one new item. A large Alcaini male hulked in front of it, in an unmistakably defensive posture. The helmet and uniform he wore bore little resemblance to the gauzy loungewear that served as Alcaini fashion. The staff he held looked like it meant business.

She blinked. "That's new," she murmured.

Ez'iri cocked her head. "What is new?"

"The man. The guard." In person, as opposed to her dream, Alcaini males had more presence than she realized. "I've never seen an Alcaini man in person before." The being in question stared straight ahead, never even hinting that he was aware of being the subject of interest. His skin remained ruddy and impassive.

Ez'iri smiled, her forked tongue flicking between pointed teeth. "Tai'en took it upon himself to ensure my protection. It is his right as a member of my family." She stood next to the second bay. "Although I suspect his curiosity about humans motivates him more than concern for my safety. This way, of your pleasure." She motioned to the third bay. "And of yours, Physician Kenneth'en."

Buhlmeier would get a kick out of the way Ez'iri mangled idiom, she thought. Ez'iri began asking her questions, interspersing them with explanations of the instruments she was lining up. The Alcaini were interested in the sensitivity of their skin, and the strength and structure of their bones. Rayne answered the questions as best as she could, noting Kenneth's nervousness.

Ez'iri noticed, too. "Your mate—he does not approve?"

She frowned. "He's not my mate. Hasn't been for years, in fact."

"My error."

The portal opened and several other Alcaini females joined them. The tone of the lead female could only be that of a teacher lecturing students. Some things were universal, Rayne thought ruefully, as she noted the bored looks on some of the faces of the rear guard.

As the examination continued, she noticed the Alcaini women shooting strange looks at their guard. During a break, she asked Ez'iri about it.

Ez'iri rolled her eyes and shrugged. "My kinsman is something of a legend among our people. No one has seen him take a mate."

"Hasn't met the right girl yet?"

Ez'iri smiled, her skin bluing with amusement. "I know how your people feel about mating. But it is not the same way my people feel. Mating is something we share. We do not hide it like a…" she searched for the word "…shame?"

"Sin, you mean."

"Yes! It is not a sin to us."

"It isn't to us, either," Kenneth interjected. "We're just private about it."

As fascinating as the Alcaini were, she couldn't comprehend this part of their culture. She would probably never again have a lover, because of her need to keep her desires private—a culture that saw things the complete opposite boggled her mind.

"Tai'en has more in common with humans in that respect. However, for us, it is a sin that he chooses not to mate."

"Shame," Rayne corrected. "Unless you mean that his not mating is a punishable offense."

"A shame, then. None would dare punish a warrior. Tai'en's decision, however shameful, still brings honor to our family, because he holds it with honor and strength."

"So you value deep convictions?" Kenneth asked.

Ez'iri frowned. "Deep...I do not understand."

It was Rayne's turn to search for words. "Tai'en will not change his ways, and it is honorable that he doesn't, even if his decision is not."

"Yes, I think that is a good explanation. Your research has undoubtedly revealed that our race does not breed easily. Frequent matings are the best way to ensure the continuation of our houses."

She and Kenneth both nodded. She had been surprised at the lack of in vitro fertilization research until Kenneth discovered that the subject was taboo. Since the Alcaini had their own solution, the research team decided they wouldn't risk offending them by bringing up the subject of human reproductive technology.

"Do you have children, Physician Ez'iri?"

Ez'iri's skin yellowed. Her eyes, alien as they were, conveyed a clear sadness. "No. But I am still in youth and have many mates who please me well."

Kenneth blushed and again, Rayne had to bite her lip to keep the laugh down. Kenneth the sex-therapist, blushing over an Alcaini turn of phrase? Who knew?

She couldn't resist shooting Tai'en glances through the rest of the discourse. When it came time for the humans to examine the Alcaini in the information exchange, her thoughts turned to Ez'iri's contradictory words. Tai'en brought disappointment on their house, but by refusing to knuckle under, he also brought honor.

Her convictions were the same. She wouldn't ever expose herself to the humiliation and hurt again, but the need for fulfillment would not silence itself.

See as a woman sees...

If her quest for fulfillment were foremost in her mind, she knew without a doubt what she'd do.

The Alcaini had technology undreamed of by humans. Simulation technology that could accurately reproduce objects that not only looked real, but felt real as well, through energized plasma.

Her gaze rested on Tai'en, the warrior too shy to mate. He radiated power. Couple that with what she knew of the Alcaini biology and—

He was the stuff of pure, heated fantasy.

Ez'iri regarded her thoughtfully. "Rayne'iri," she said, "What is it about my kinsman that fascinates you so?"

She snapped out of her thoughts abruptly. A blush burned its way up her cheeks, causing her to nearly match Alcaini coloring. "I—he…" she stammered, then sighed. "Your kinsman sounds a lot like me. I, too, am very selective of my mates. In fact, I fear there's no one on Earth who could 'please me well' to use your words. I've even stopped looking."

"That is reason to look even more forcefully, I think. Were I to have your problem, I would stop at nothing to find a mate."

"I don't know if it's that important." Rayne laughed, but inwardly she cringed.

"Oh, but it is," Ez'iri said earnestly. "There is nothing more important than fulfilling the desire for a mate."

Now there's a woman in touch with her biological urges, Rayne thought. Could she really live the rest of her life with a hungering need and no means to feed it? Or would it grow with time, until for want of satisfaction, it consumed her? "I will not allow myself to be hurt again. Protecting my heart overrides my need to have a lover," she said firmly.

Ez'iri's words returned again to haunt her the next day. The Alcaini way of thinking enticed her. She'd never before considered sex a top priority, and now she wondered why. If she were Alcaini, like Ez'iri, she would stop at nothing to find her fulfillment.

She thought so hard about it that she finally indulged in a little fantasy. If she were Alcaini, what would she do?

Find an Alcaini man, for one thing. But the impossibilities surrounding that one didn't even come close to being overcome. She remembered the hot yearning of her dream of a few nights ago, the slick feel of penetrating fullness her mind inspired with the sight of the Alcaini male and the poor substitute made by her fingers.

What about two men at once? Maybe it was time to reconsider that option. But how could she find not one, but two men who would accommodate her? How could she risk exposing her needs, baring herself, and being outnumbered?

Toys? Her fingers had been poor shadows of what could be. She owned a little-used vibrator completely lacking in inspiration. No, she wanted something— someone more responsive than a vulcanized rubber dong without even a man attached to it.

If only I could find a pair of androids...

The thought came out of nowhere and hit her like a ton of bricks. The Alcaini had androids! Or those plasma-generated automatons. They looked real, felt real, and acted plenty real—if the startled looks on their faces when she first woke up in the Alcaini med lab gave any indication.

Ez'iri's words pounded relentlessly at her. *Stop at nothing...*

The Alcaini dream man added his words. *See as a woman sees...*

She remembered the yellow, sad flush of Ez'iri's skin at the mention of children. The Alcaini woman must be heartbroken, in spite of her words to the contrary. If it weren't for that stupid taboo—

Her eyes narrowed. It was a risky plan, the one forming in her mind, but once coalesced, she couldn't talk herself out of it. Almost as if her hunger, her need had caught her napping, and shoved her aside to take control.

She contacted Ez'iri. *I have a solution to get us both what we want. Meet me at the transport tonight. Tell no one.*

The warehouse crawled with shadows. If she were caught, she'd be fired or maybe worse…tampering with the delicate relations between humanity and a technologically superior race for the sake of an orgasm went beyond insane. Yet here she was.

"Hsst!" Ez'iri's eyes suddenly appeared, glowing in the darkness beside her. "What is the secrecy?" Her voice was amused. "Have you asked me here about my kinsman? I have been viewing your video entertainment. It seems you humans have an inordinate preoccupation with the rituals leading up to mating."

Rayne grimaced in the dark. "Please don't judge us by our entertainment." She thought of Tai'en, that lean power, barely contained. "I don't ask about your kinsman, but I do ask about a man."

"Your ex-mate, then?"

"Hell, no!" God, if Kenneth ever got wind of this, he'd have her committed. Under his observation, of course, so he could get the grant money and write more papers on her. She modulated her tone to a more reasonable pitch. "No. I think I've found a solution in my search for a mate. And you can help me get it."

"This interests me. How?"

"Those plasma generators that you used to create simulations of yourselves to study us."

Ez'iri's eyes flashed. "That is advanced technology we aren't permitted to share."

"I know, and believe me, I won't. But isn't there some way you could get a small one? Just a simple one, with a simple program of an Alcaini male?"

"You wish to mate with an Alcaini? Our mating practices are…"

"Yes, I know all that. Your mating practices are harsh and could cause damage to a human. But this is what I want. What I need." As an afterthought, she added, "It wouldn't hurt if the simulation did bear some resemblance to your kinsman."

"But—a simulation? It is…" Ez'iri's voice dropped to a whisper, even though it was dark and they were alone "…No one would even consider it. There would be no chance of a child—a waste."

"Humans have a lot more sex for pleasure than Alcaini do. We don't have as many problems with fertility. Which brings me to our next subject." She held up a data stick, knowing that Ez'iri could see it perfectly, even in the pitch-dark.

"What is it?"

"Information," Rayne said, fear tightening her belly. If Ez'iri took offense at her next words, the world might end. "On human techniques of assisted reproduction."

"Assist…" Ez'iri's voice trailed off. Her eyes flashed again. "Rayne'iri, you are human, so I will forgive you this insult. But we shall not speak of this ever again." The Alcaini woman's voice was harsh.

Instead of taking the out offered, Rayne pressed on, fully aware that she was now on the grounds of an Incident of Intergalactic Proportions. "Did you not counsel me to stop at nothing to achieve my desire?"

Ez'iri growled. "This is not similar."

"Yes, it is. There is information here that could help you have a child. I want you to have it." She dropped her tone. "You are my friend, and you are hurting. And it is not the human way to let a friend hurt."

"I will leave you now," Ez'iri said.

More attuned to sounds in the complete blackness, Rayne heard the absence of the harsh edge to her alien friend's voice, but wisely chose not to comment.

Ez'iri disappeared back into the transfer point, vanishing completely without a sound, the only evidence of her absence the sudden disappearance of her gleaming alien eyes.

Chapter Three

Rayne locked the door of the rendezvous warehouse behind her. Her footsteps echoed in the cavernous room, empty save for the transfer module. She flicked on a small penlight.

There on the transfer pad stood a small box, looking a bit like a compact disc player. Her heart suddenly slammed in her chest. *She really did it*, Rayne thought. *She really went through with it.*

She took the unit from the transfer pad and replaced it with a data stick. "Begin transfer," she said, aiming her penlight at the pad.

Before her eyes, the data stick dissolved and disappeared. She forced herself not to think about her own body, having done that several times already. It gave her a huge case of stomach butterflies.

Butterflies that would have crowded the ones already present in her stomach. Her body felt weak, liquid. She couldn't believe she'd gone so far—pushed so many limits and made so many risky decisions for something that most people wouldn't have bothered with. She was insane.

No, she thought, just driven. The Alcaini understood.

Ez'iri's communiqué had come after a three-day silence during which Rayne fully expected to be arrested every time someone so much as said "boo" to her. Two more visits to the Alcaini had been scheduled for the team and neither had mentioned her.

She thought for sure she'd blown it, until the encoded communiqué showed up in her inbox. Ez'iri's message was short and to the point, but still contained the sensual fluidity characteristic of Alcaini language. *Your determination is admirable, and you seduce me with my own words. Let not the unorthodox methods of culmination diminish the honor of the strength of our twin purposes. Fulfill your desires at the following time and place, as will I, after which we may exchange the sources of our solutions once again, with never another cognizant.*

In short, meet me at the drop at midnight.

Ez'iri's terms were strict. They would exchange information for technology, but only for a limited time. Rayne's hunger would be fulfilled, but only one glorious time. She would return the unit to Ez'iri, and her Alcaini friend would return the information, unrecorded, to her.

"Run program Male Alcaini One," she commanded.

Ez'iri's voice greeted her. "Rayne'iri, I have programmed what you requested. This unit is small, well-used, and will not be missed for a few hours. However, the technology is aged. The program is not sophisticated, but should meet your—needs." Ez'iri's voice trilled with amusement. "I have programmed the unit to adjust according to your physiology, but you must still use caution. The power cell will last one quarter of an hour. Take your pleasure, my friend."

The unit began to glow with a soft, silvery light, as if captured starlight lurked somewhere in the box. From the port, a pale, amorphous blob of plasma emerged, shooting up about six feet and gradually coalescing into a humanoid shape. Her eyes dropped to what hung between his legs.

The irresistible urge to sing "Take me out to the ball game" made her grimace and laugh at the same time. The old joke about how a guy could walk with four balls alternately had no humor at all, yet seemed more hysterical than it ever had before. The pit of her stomach fluttered and a blush heated her cheeks, spreading down her neck to the tops of her breasts beneath the lab coat she'd hastily thrown on to retrieve her package. Four balls, she thought. Batter, take your base.

But more than the four balls that hung between his legs was the rest of the equipment. Not one, but two cocks hung, heavy and somnolent. Sleeping beasts born in the sky, to assuage an earthy, yet unearthly hunger.

She licked her lips. What woman wouldn't go wet and weak-kneed over a man with two cocks?

She turned away from the unit's soft glow, checking the blackness of the warehouse for any signs of life.

Nothing disrupted the dark, save for the glow. Wait—
She tensed, the pit of her stomach dropping.

No. The brief spark at the edge of the light cast
from the unit was an illusion, an afterimage from the
movement of light to dark and back again. She sighed,
the imagined brush with discovery both scaring her and,
astonishingly, exciting her.

As she walked back towards her coalescing fantasy
lover, dampness slicked her inner lips and trickled
between her thighs. Her nipples tightened in
anticipation.

Finally, after an eternity, he was solid.

Wordlessly, he came to her. Damn, she thought.
Ez'iri knew her better than she thought. The "passing
resemblance" to her kinsman was the understatement of
the century.

"Come here, secret fantasy lover," she said, feeling
free to indulge in a little over-emotive dialogue, away
from prying eyes. "There's no one around to watch our
little secret."

She opened her mouth for his kiss. He rubbed his
alien tongue against hers in a slow, deliberate rhythm
that blossomed into an echoing heartbeat between her
legs. The cool, smooth skin of his fingers stroked her
body, and she put her hands over his, guiding his hands
to cup her breasts.

He seemed to know what to do then, letting his
thumbs graze her nipples. She pushed his head down to
her chest. "Take one in your mouth," she commanded
breathlessly.

He did so, stroking his rough tongue across the sensitive flesh. The ache between her legs intensified. She'd had enough foreplay. She pushed him down further.

The program, however, in its sophistication of learning and adapting to external stimuli, resisted. He focused on her other nipple, laving it with his tongue until she squirmed. When she commanded, "Down," he snapped his sharp teeth down on her lightly. The pleasure-pain sent a wave of dizziness through her.

Finally—oh, finally—he knelt before her and ran his hands up the insides of her thighs, his thick fingers parting her lips, dipping inside for the briefest of moments before emerging, dewy-wet, to stroke her aching clit. "God, please," she begged, feeling the blood rush from her head to her crotch.

He pushed a finger inside her slick channel. Her inner muscles contracted as he slid deeper. And the yearning welled up inside her, that unfulfilled hollowness that soon—please, oh, soon—would finally be filled.

He stroked in and out, stoking her, winding her tight until she knew she'd explode. Shudders wracked her body and a mini-orgasm swept over her.

"No!" she cried out in frustration. The throbbing in her pussy sent signals of fulfillment on heartbeats to her brain and the rest of her body, but the off-beats echoed the opposite. The aching void that needed to be filled.

He stood. "We are not through, lady," he said in halting English.

She blinked. Ez'iri had said this was old tech. Old her naked ass! He came with a working English vocabulary! The Alcaini truly were an advanced civilization. *Ez'iri, you gem.*

The specimen of that advanced civilization pushed her down to her knees with one forceful, but solicitous motion and she found herself nose to nuts with his two twitching members.

She'd always enjoyed giving head as an amusing diversion, a way to while away the time on the way to an orgasm. But this—this would be a challenge. She licked her lips and bent her head.

She ran her tongue around the swollen head of his forecock. The hot slickness of his flesh seemed to warm her from above, even as her knees protested the chill cement of the bare floor.

He sucked in a breath. His skin began to darken, from a pale ruddiness to an exotic lavender. She didn't expect Ez'iri to have bothered to include that detail in her programming. She closed her lips over the head and moved them up and down. The scent of him surrounded her, a mixture of musk, wood, and heat from a distant star.

He groaned. "Your…hand, Lady. Use your hand." He guided her hand to his aft shaft. A quick study, she began stroking it, testing the rhythms and his reaction. He liked it when she used alternating rhythms, bobbing her head down while stroking up with her hand, tonguing the tip of the fore while her fingers encircled the base of the aft.

She switched, tilting her head sideways to tongue the base of his aft cock while she stroked the fore. "Can I—hold them together?" she asked. Why was she worried about pleasing a plasma construct anyway?

He nodded. "Carefully." He showed her how to cup her hands around both of his shafts. Only the tips could touch, but the effect sent her reeling anyway. She opened her mouth wide and closed her lips around the two heads.

"Yesss…" he hissed, his forked tongue darting out from between his lips. She'd forgotten about the tongue. Oh, if only she could have more than fifteen stolen minutes to explore the exotic possibilities of that tongue! "You humans are very creative."

Funny he should say that. Almost as if he had a consciousness of his own. Surely not. Surely even the Alcaini didn't have that kind of technology. They would be gods.

He pulled away and knelt in front of her. "Turn around that I may fulfill your desires, Lady."

This was it. This was what she'd been waiting for. Her stomach clenched and her thighs quivered as she turned around, falling to her hands and knees.

She felt his hands on her back, sliding up along her spine to push her shoulders down onto the ground. Her ass jutted in the air. She felt herself opening, fore and aft, ready for what only he could give.

His hands slid back down along her flanks. His fingers parted her ass cheeks, exposing her to the cool air, which now carried her own spicy feminine musk. The blunt head of his rear shaft probed at the entrance of her vagina. Slowly, achingly slowly, he eased the head into her pussy. She panted, guessing—knowing what came next.

Her rear muscles flexed, her taut tightness gave way to the blunt probing of his forecock. The hollow ache turned greedy. "Please," she begged.

He began to move gently and the sensation was incredible. At the same time, it was not enough. The feel of two cocks, sliding simultaneously in and out of her, sent shockwaves of pleasure tingling through her entire lower body. Her breasts ached and she cupped them, laying her cheek on the ground as she massaged her nipples.

Her hunger grew and she began, tentatively, to push back against him, shifting her hips this way and that until she found a rhythm that felt right. Soon she bucked her hips, groaning and arching backwards, needing more, more, more.

He was holding back. She sensed it. God, was the program that sensitive? She tossed her hair back and glared at him over her shoulder. "Harder," she commanded.

His pace remained maddeningly steady. All she could do was rock back and meet his thrusts. His fingers danced a rhythm down the lower half of her spine, around her hips, and back up her flanks. It felt soothing. She didn't want soothing. She groaned, frustration and pleasure tightening her chest. "Faster, please." She punctuated her demands with sharp arches of her hips.

He hunched over her, changing his angle of penetration, but not his pace.

"Dammit," she muttered. Now she couldn't even push back.

His breath was hot on the back of her neck. "Human physiology is too fragile to accept the full thrust of Alcaini mating practices."

Unbelievable! Her body strung taut like a bow, quivering on the insane edge of the yawning pit of the deepest orgasm she'd ever know, and the program defaulted to a biology lesson—with puns? Was there nothing—no force in the entire universe—that could fulfill one simple, basic need of one human woman? She tossed her head back and growled low in her throat, a primal, animal sound.

The hips thrusting against hers slowed. The cocks sliding in and out of her stilled. The fingers stopped their dance and gripped firmly. "Human physiology..." he began, although the program must have experienced a power surge, because the vocals trembled.

"Fuck the biology lesson," she snarled. Her body vibrated. Her very soul stretched towards the shimmering scalpel-edge where universe and chaos met and split. "Override the safety measures. I want—I need all of it!"

His fingers resumed their movement, this time more roughly, his nails rasping along her flesh. He started moving again, this time thrusting harder, faster. She bucked back against him and he responded in kind. Finally, he filled her all the way, his two cocks working in synchronous motion, dragging back and forth against her inner walls, one slickly wet, the other accepting him with delicious friction. She moaned and growled satisfaction at the same time, if that were possible.

The sounds incited him further. Her body opened, stretched to its limit. Blood rushed to her swollen clit, away from her brain. She grew dizzy as her fingers dug into the unyielding floor for purchase against the powerful force taking her out to the furthest reaches of the universe. Her muscles screamed, protesting the ferocious pace of his thrusts, but pleasure rode over the pain, mingling with it to form a heady elixir that made her embrace every sensation. Her vision behind her closed eyelids expanded. Her orgasm exploded not over her, but from deep within her, sending her consciousness out with an interstellar wail that echoed through light years. Her channel clenched, her hips arched involuntarily.

And she felt him, a roar that began in his chest and vibrated through his body, bubbling from his balls to his throat as his fingers raked up her tensed spine to her shoulders and pushed her flat on the ground. He covered her body with his. His hot breath fanned the sensitive nape of her neck as her hair fell forward.

She felt his mouth on her skin, then the sharp nip of his teeth. She cried out, the pain sending a second shockwave of pleasure through her body, threatening to shake her to pieces with the sheer sensation of it.

Then he exploded, pulsating twin fountains filling and quieting the aching need deep inside of her.

Her heart slammed in her chest. The cold cement of the bare floor met her heated body in a sharp and almost painful meeting of fire and ice. Her body felt flushed and full—fulfilled. Sweat dampened her where his body touched hers, followed by a cooling breeze as he withdrew.

She lay there for a full minute, gathering the various bits of herself back from the dark edges of the universe. Then she rolled over. She stretched languidly and looked at her male specimen.

He crouched on the ground, his head down. His body no longer held the violet hue of Alcaini sexual arousal, but rather a deep, apple-red ruddiness. Her scientist's mind fastened on this observation and marveled at the technology that must have gone into the plasma-generator program.

Speaking of the plasma generator—she reluctantly reached for her lab coat. Every move she made sent aftershocks of pleasure shooting from her clit out to her extremities as she stood up and took the required two steps towards the unit. Her reaction to bending over brought her to her knees, her hands clutching the soft fabric of the garment as another mini-orgasm swept over her. It felt like her internal organs completely rewired themselves to attach to the pleasure-sensation part of her brain so that every movement, every shift of her body, triggered her pleasure center again and again.

Creamy wetness clung to the tops of her inner thighs. She tucked a piece of the coat hem in between her legs and pressed the fabric against her vulva to stop the throbbing for just a minute while she got her head together. She needed to think and she couldn't do that while orgasmic ricochets bounced her brain around in bubbling hormone soup.

She fished in her pocket and brought out her penlight and her watch. Twenty minutes had passed since she activated the program. She frowned. "Fascinating," she murmured. Maybe like everything else Alcaini, they just worked better than expected.

Ez'iri would be waiting for the unit's return.

Her body slowly quieted, the pause between aftershocks growing longer. She finally felt ready to try for the walk to the transfer station. Still shaky, but rallying, she made her way to the compartment. Thank heavens no one was around to see her like this.

The glow faded from the tubes of gel-like substance that powered the plasma generator, indicating that the fuel in the cells had exhausted itself. Her fantasy lover was gone forever.

Her stomach knotted. Now that she knew what completion felt like, could she settle for never having it again?

She would have to. She wasn't about to risk herself with another lover. The men she knew thought of her as cold, her formidable mind intimidating. Kenneth thought of her as a research project—a test subject to be studied in a lab.

The plasma generator allowed her fulfillment without the vulnerability. Her Alcaini lover, no matter how solid and responsive, remained nothing more than a construct of electrically charged plasma, with a highly sophisticated program determining his—its—behavior. "He's not real," she murmured aloud. Odd, though, how a plasma construct could have such presence. A presence that lingered even after she knew she was alone.

She placed the unit in the transfer station. This was it. Oh, but it was tempting to keep the unit—steal it, hide it, anything to repeat that intense, risk-free gratification. But betraying Ez'iri's trust was one step further than she was willing to take. "Begin transfer." Her forlorn command echoed through the room.

All that remained was to clean up the evidence that she'd been using the warehouse, and to clean up herself—a hot bath was high on the agenda—and she could continue with life. No messy morning afters, no post-coital awkwardness. Everything wrapped up nice and tidy.

The transfer pad chimed softly, indicating an incoming. She pointed her penlight at it. The data stick lay on the pad, and the only evidence of her adventure was the drenched ache between her legs.

The ache subsided as she hiked back across the compound to her quarters, leaving her with a pleasant exhaustion, rather like a hard workout. In spite of the cool humidity of late night, her body still burned. She turned the climate controls down as soon as she got in the door.

Suddenly thirsty, she headed straight for the refrigerator, bypassing a glass in favor of chugging fruit juice straight from the bottle. *If good sex leaves you this worn-out, I've never had it in all my thirty-four years*, she thought.

She took the bottle of juice into the bathroom with her and turned on the tub faucet. While the tub filled, she collected the candles and scented soap and oils she only brought out for special occasions. A nice, relaxing hot bath to soothe her muscles, and then a long, deep sleep—all weekend, if necessary—was all she wanted out of life.

Once the candles were lit, she turned out the vanity light and shrugged out of the lab coat. As she turned towards the tub, she caught a look at her naked body in the mirror and stopped, mesmerized by what she saw.

Her hair stood out in its usual wild mass of copper curls. Even dampened in the warm humid air of the bathroom, her hair still found the fortitude to defy gravity. But the rest of her looked different.

She peered into the gently fogging mirror. She had the look of a woman well-satisfied. Even the thought made her blush faintly. The last thing she'd ever do would be to walk around in public with a look like that. No one—especially Kenneth—could be allowed to see her like this.

The wound on her shoulder stood out, a ruddy crescent moon on her pale skin. Lack of sleep produced dark circles under her eyes, making them more luminous than their usual lead-gray. A well-satisfied look certainly didn't come from there, although her eyes were a bit—softer than usual.

Her lips, maybe. Her lips were puffy from his kisses and her own biting.

She gave up trying to figure out where the Look came from and sank into the bath.

And leaped right back out of it with a yelp. "What the…" She checked the temperature setting on the tap. One-oh-two, same as always.

She shook her head, puzzled, and adjusted the bath water temperature ten degrees southward. Cool water spouted from the faucet and automatically shut off when the temperature evened out.

"Ahh, much better," she said aloud. She closed her eyes and let the tepid water close over her exhausted body.

Gradually, she became aware of a free-floating sensation. She floated above her body, slowly turning to gaze at herself, a distant, mild amazement the only emotion she could muster. How peaceful she looked, lying there. Her nipples floated above the water. They should be cold, she thought.

Her body heard her, and responded, the dusky peaks pebbling. The water lapped at the shores of her breasts. Her Alcaini lover had lapped the same way. She remembered his tongue. Alien, forked, capable of inciting intense pleasures she hadn't even begun to explore. Pleasure tightened, coiled in her lower midsection. Even recently sated, the hunger still held the promise of what it could become.

She looked down on herself, aroused by memory and sensation, watching a pale violet flush creep up the valley of her breasts and spread across her abdomen. She was dreaming, of course, she realized with a start. Alcaini blushed violet with sexual arousal, not humans.

Suddenly dry-lipped, she licked her lips. In the bath below, the dream-Rayne's tongue darted out, sleek and forked. Her eyes opened, revealing not their usual nickel-patina, but the topaz glow of Alcaini.

She gasped. Thrashing around, she slammed back into herself, now down in the bath, terrified fingers reaching between her lips to feel for her tongue, her blessedly normal, mushy, unforked, *human* tongue.

She jumped out of the bath, examining her arms and her chest for traces of violet hue. Nothing but pink and the occasional freckle. Jesus.

Naked and dripping wet, she turned towards the mirror. Same gray eyes as always. Nothing even remotely alien about them.

She drew in a shaky breath and reached for a towel. Teeth chattering, she mopped her face and wound the thick terry cloth around her body. For one fear-crazed instant, she thought about calling Kenneth. She immediately realized the short trip to the insane asylum that call would produce and nixed the idea.

She was probably just having a reaction to the fantasy—that was all. There were emotional implications to having alien sex, going beyond the biology. Kenneth's whole "we can, but we shouldn't" argument covered those points comprehensively.

"But it wasn't real," she told herself out loud.

Maybe not, but her mind could think it was. She reached for the bottle of juice and took a long swallow, surprised to realize it was almost gone.

Still unnerved and shaken, she checked her skin, face, and mouth two more times before finally leaving the bathroom. Perhaps it was a good thing she only had the unit the one time. Repeated episodes like this one were liable to send her screaming into the nuthouse.

She crawled wearily under the covers of her bed and closed her eyes. Her body might be replete, but her mind just wouldn't let it go.

An hour of futile tossing and turning netted her zero sleep, so she abandoned the effort and instead flicked on the computer.

An encoded communiqué from Ez'iri awaited her. She smiled. Her alien friend's sense of humor would no doubt insist she send some wicked double-edged comments on the success of their exchange.

She decoded and opened it. As she read the message, her mild amusement gave way to full-blown panic.

My deepest apologies to you, my friend Physician Rayne'iri. The data you sent me is of excellent quality, but I am dishonored to discover that the plasma generator unit I sent you was inoperable. Please grant me the occasion to restore honor to our friendship in person and come to me upon reading this message.

"Ohmigodohmigodno," she murmured, pushing her fisted knuckles against her lips. The daydream, the night's events, her hours-long reassurances to herself all jumbled together to send her into mild hysteria.

Her fantasy lover, the incredible sex, her mind-blowing orgasms—

It was all real.

Chapter Four

Her clinical detachment, her razor-sharp scientist's mind, her professional demeanor, all deserted her, leaving her lizard brain to cope with the monumental reality of having just had sex with an alien. She fled from the computer, desperate to be anywhere but where Ez'iri's words could haunt her.

She made it as far as the kitchen. Maybe Ez'iri was mistaken. She had seen the unit spewing out plasma. Surely no Alcaini male would want to mate with a human—there wasn't even the remotest chance of conception! Least of all, Ez'iri's kinsman, Tai'en. If he was picky by Alcaini standards, how could a human woman stand a chance?

Evidence. She should look for evidence before meeting Ez'iri. *Don't panic*, she told herself, more than a little belatedly. Instead, she filled the sink with cold water and plunged her head into it, unwilling to chance another hallucinogenic trip into the bathtub.

God, the way she'd acted! Wanton, animalistic. She held her breath under the icy water for as long as she could, then burst up straight.

Water streamed from her face and hair, puddling on the kitchen floor. Her stomach churned and she needed a drink. It was downright shameful the way she'd dropped to her hands and knees and begged to be mounted.

An unexpected wave of heat flooded her and once again, she felt that deep, quivering feeling of aftershock, as if her pleasure center were over stimulated.

She wrapped her arms around her midsection. No! It wasn't worth it. Humiliation drove away the brief resurgence of sexual energy, leaving her feeling exposed, ashamed.

Her throat choked up and sudden tears burned her eyelids. It couldn't be true. If another person witnessed her, knew her vulnerability like that—she wanted to die.

She used two hands to scoop water from the sink and gulp it down her throat. Somebody—Tai'en—betrayed her. Used the technology to deceive her.

Why?

A light tapping at her front door interrupted her soak-and-panic routine. She buried her face in a dishtowel for a long minute, then went to the door. Through the peephole, she spied Kenneth, shifting from one foot to the other. She opened the door a crack.

"Hello, Rayne."

"What are you doing here, Kenneth?"

"I—can I come in?"

She bit her lip. If anyone could sense there was something wrong with her, it would be Kenneth. She closed her eyes briefly. "It's late."

"I know. I brought you something." He pulled a green bottle out of a paper sack. She squinted at the label, recognizing the gold foiling and picture of a brand of champagne that she couldn't usually afford.

"What are you up to?" There had to be a reason he was bringing her gifts. Fortunately, a champagne bottle was a little small to be hiding a Greek army inside it. She pushed the door open a little further, revealing herself in all her wet nightshirted glory.

Kenneth's eyes traveled down and back up her body. She folded her arms over her breasts as she stood back to let him in. "That's not yours to look at anymore."

He had the grace to blush. "Sorry. I couldn't help it. You're a very attractive woman."

She pushed the door closed and padded down the hall to don her robe. "Save it for someone who hasn't heard that line before. There are glasses in the cupboard above the stove."

A minute later, she heard a pop, then the fizz of bubbly. She paused before leaving her bedroom. Ez'iri's message still graced her computer screen. She typed a quick reply.

My friend—I had a wonderful time with the unit. You must be mistaken. Let's meet tomorrow.

Looking at the words on the screen, her inner panic subsided to a dull, nagging worry. Yes. Ez'iri was mistaken. The unit must have broken after she'd used it. She never did trust those transfer stations one hundred percent. She hit send and returned to the living room and a waiting Kenneth.

He handed her champagne. "Cheers," he said.

"Bottoms up," she returned, the irony not completely lost on her. The champagne tickled all the way down her throat, hitting her stomach with a dry, tart swash. She closed her eyes for a moment, savoring the rush of warmth the alcohol sent racing through her system. "Now what brings you to my door with booze that I'd have to take a loan out to buy?"

Kenneth led her to the couch and settled her before taking his own seat on the opposite end. "It's a peace offering," he said. "I was wrong to do what I did to you. I simply couldn't fathom the thought that you needed more than I could give you. I had to prove there was a psychological reason behind the disintegration of our relationship."

She took another sip of champagne, staring over his shoulder to the window that dominated the far wall. He'd thrown the drapes open to let in the light of the crescent moon and the myriad stars. One of those stars, a tiny prick of light, was the Alcaini ship.

"This is all very sudden, don't you think?" Kenneth's abrupt willingness to admit his wrongdoing, after two years of insisting he did nothing wrong and riding on the laurels of it, set off her internal alarms. On the other hand, her panic about Ez'iri's dire warning seemed to be shifting back into blessed perspective.

He looked down for a minute, staring into the bottom of his champagne glass. When he looked up, his expression was warm and held excitement. "There is another reason," he admitted.

Feeling vindicated didn't give her the thrill she thought it would. Probably because once again, humanity—in the form of Kenneth—disappointed her.

"Have another drink of champagne and I'll tell you."

Curious, and because it wasn't a hardship, she obeyed. She was feeling quite warm and sparkly by the time he spoke again. "You've been chosen as the most likely candidate, you see, for a new experiment." He scooted closer. "It's top-secret, but the ramifications are astounding."

An experiment. "Another experiment? I'm not sure that's an honor," she said. "Am I going to see more completely off-base theories about my sexual proclivities in print?"

He grimaced. "Rayne, did you even read that paper?"

"Yes I did." In spite of Ez'iri's disturbing mistake, her experience had shown her without a doubt that her intellect in no way inhibited her sexuality—her chosen partners did. A wry smile twisted her lips. "I can say with great confidence that your theory was well-thought out, firmly supported, and utter and complete fiction."

He moved closer. "Really. How can you be sure? How many lovers have you had since we were together? Have any of them been able to satisfy you? No, because your intellect won't allow you the satisfaction of letting a purely physical reaction take the lead."

She took another drink of her wine. The urge to confide in him gripped her. Seeing the smug look of righteousness fall off his face would be right on par with a multiple orgasm right now. "As a matter of fact…"

No! She had to keep her mouth shut, or she and Ez'iri both could suffer from their illicit exchange.

"You can tell me," Kenneth said with an engaging smile. "I'm a doctor."

That did it. She refused to be patronized to any longer. "You're a schmuck." Loose-tongued from the champagne, she said, "The Alcaini don't think there's anything wrong with me at all."

He looked suddenly interested. "Really? What makes you say that?"

Now she'd done it. She said too much. She tried to make her fogged brain come up with something convincing but nowhere near her actual experiences. Her earlier discussion with Ez'iri came to the rescue. "My standards are high. The Alcaini respect dedication to one's principles." As an afterthought, she added, "You were there."

"Somehow, I don't think you're telling me everything."

"Too bad." She tossed back the rest of her champagne. "So tell me more about this experiment you volunteered me for." As she put her empty glass on the coffee table, she caught the flash of a yellow glow out of the corner of her eye, through the window. "Hmm," she muttered. "Fireflies must be out."

He turned towards the window with a nervous start. "Where?"

She flopped back on the couch. "Outside." Thinking no more about it, she let herself enjoy the warm lassitude that made even waving her hand an effort. "Forget about it."

"How are you feeling?"

She raised an eyebrow. "That's a dumb question coming from such a smart guy who just—plied me with half a bottle of Moet."

"So you're pretty relaxed, would you say?"

"Quit trying to be my shrink," she said. "And don't even th—think about trying anything—I'm about to kick you out."

"Sure, sure, I'll be gone in just a few minutes."

Through hazy eyes, she saw him draw something from his shirt pocket. "What's that?"

She realized with some trepidation that it took effort to follow the path his hand was making towards her. He held a slim wand in his fingers that she realized was a hypodermic injector, the kind normally used to administer emergency allergy shots.

"Shh, Rayne. I told you. You're the candidate we've selected for our insurance policy."

She tried to move. She threw every ounce of energy into rising from the couch. All she managed to do was flop forward over the coffee table. "Wha'd y' slip me, y'bastard?"

"Just a little sedative. It'll wear off in a few hours."

"Wha'y'mean, 'insurance pol'cy?'" Her fingers. Her fingers were moving towards the bottle of champagne. Idly, she noticed his glass sat untouched on the far edge of the table. Dirty bastard, she thought.

"The Alcaini are obviously technologically advanced. But they still have weaknesses." He moved her hair away from her neck. "These microbes have been bio-engineered against what we know of Alcaini physiology. When the Alcaini attempt to take over our world, we'll stop them by activating the microbes." His fingers brushed against a small sore spot where her Alcaini lover had bitten her. Back when the world was normal.

Alcaini, taking over the world. "Dumbest thin' I ever heard," she mumbled. Her fingers made another agonizing inch's progress towards the champagne bottle. "Alcaini're peaceful. They've already got a world of their own."

He pressed the hypo against her skin. "No race that actively explores beyond its boundaries is truly peaceful. When activated, these microbes will use your body as a delivery system to distribute a neuro-toxin deadly to Alcaini physiology. Once everyone aboard that ship is dead and the immediate threat is over, we can exploit their technology and create better defenses against them." He pushed the plunger.

The spring-loaded needle bit into her skin and she cried out with the sudden pain of it. Her fingers found the bottle. "You sumbitch!" With all her strength, she swung the bottle towards his head.

It bounced off. "Ow," he said, jerking away from her. "That wasn't nice, pet." He slid over to the other side of the couch. "Now I'll just wait here for a few minutes while the microbes make their merry way through your system. It won't hurt much, I'm told. But it will make your bodily fluids toxic to Alcaini."

The heaviness of the torpor in her limbs faded, replaced by an equally paralyzing burning sensation radiating out from the wound in her neck to her entire torso. Her vision greyed out for a moment and her fingers and toes began to tingle. Her eyes watered, and not entirely from a purely physical reaction. "Y'r killing me, Ken," she forced the words from a throat that felt like it would close completely in a matter of minutes.

"You won't die right away, Rayne," he said, his tone projecting comfort that she'd never feel. "Unfortunately, after the neuro-toxin takes effect on the Alcaini, we can't guarantee your safety."

"Why me?" Her voice was barely a whisper now.

"You have the longest relationship with them. They *trust* you," he said simply. "I confirmed that during our visit to their craft."

How could she have been existing in such a Pollyanna world, she wondered. How could she have truly believed in the noble motivations of her fellow humans? She was worse than stupid, worse than vulnerable, and now she and an entire crew of well-intentioned aliens would suffer for that naiveté.

Unable to move, on hands and knees splayed over the coffee table, she would gladly have traded this exposed position for one involving an Alcaini. Ez'iri's message didn't hold nearly the threat as it had twenty minutes ago.

Oh, God, Ez'iri! Her friend would expect to see her. She had to find a way to avoid going to the Alcaini ship again!

Think, Rayne, she commanded herself. She might not be able to move, but she could still think. If Kenneth and whomever he was working for intended her to be a weapon, they had to have some means of delivering her to their target.

Kenneth petted her hair. "You know, Rayne, I rather enjoy having you here like this." His hand slid down her back to her ass. He patted her rump affectionately while she glared daggers at him. "I wonder if I could make your body respond when your mind is too busy to restrict it." His hand massaged little circles over the thin material of her robe.

"Try it," she ground out. "Maybe I'll infect you first."

He smiled, then leaned back. "I don't think so. You're too much of a cold bitch." He pulled a small wireless phone from his pocket and pressed a few keys. "I tried everything with you—things other women would go over the moon for. Nothing was good enough for you, though. That's when I realized the problem was yours, not mine."

His words were hateful, and stung, in spite of the fact that she very clearly loathed him right now, and would go to her grave—however soon that might be—despising him above all others.

The fireflies outside the window returned. Two of them, hovering together, regarding her as she regarded them. They reminded her of Alcaini eyes, gleaming golden. If she could feel her lips, she would have smiled. "Probl'm *was* y'rs," she slurred. "'lcaini got twice wha' you got. Know how t' use 't, too."

"What? You..." His face turned purple, then pale. Whatever he was about to say was cut off by the shrill chirp of his phone. He answered it quickly. "Taggart."

Her tongue felt thick and dry. Her belly burned. Outside, the fireflies inexplicably remained in hover mode and she focused on them. Wait—her toes and fingers began to tingle. The tingle spread through her body, returning feeling in a hot-cold rush of pain that brought more tears to her eyes.

Kenneth's voice interrupted her internal inventory. "I have her here. The paralysis will only last long enough to get her to the transfer station and on board the Alcaini ship."

Kenneth must have miscalculated the effects of the drugs he'd slipped her. Trust him to go for the dramatic effect while fudging it on the clinicals. For once, she was grateful his ego kept him from questioning his own cunning.

Experimentally, she tried moving her fingers. The effort caused pain to shoot up to her elbow, but her fingers closed readily. Ha! She could move.

He hung up. "There now, pet. Any last words?"

Now was her chance. If she could surprise him... "Die slow 'nd painf'l, y'numb fuck."

He glared at her. "That honor, my dear, is reserved for you." With that, he took the empty bottle and brought it down on her head.

So much for having the last word, was her last thought as stars exploded behind her eyes. Then everything went black.

* ~ *

She came to in the warehouse. Kenneth and another man were at the transfer station's pad. They'd dumped her unceremoniously on the floor, next to a stack of boxes. Her nightshirt and robe were gone, leaving her completely nude on the cold cement floor.

She put an alarmed hand down to between her legs, terrified that she'd been raped while unconscious. No moisture but her own internal humidity met her fingers, but the sudden movement sent pain hammering at her joints.

Now was her chance! She had to escape, to keep Kenneth and his companion from transferring their human bomb to the Alcaini ship.

Where could she go, on the run and completely naked?

Who cares, just go!

She rose slowly, unsteadily, but quietly, to her feet. Every muscle ached, and her limbs twitched and trembled with the effort it cost her to pull herself upright.

She made her way to the door on shaking legs that screamed in pain and yanked the door open. Behind

her, she heard Kenneth's startled shout. "Holy—sh—
Stop her!" She ignored it and fled clumsily into the
night, aiming for the thick copse of trees that served as
a picnic area for the complex's workers on break.

The door slammed open behind her just as she
reached the trees. She darted to her right, hoping to
throw them off, but barked her shin solidly against what
must have been the picnic table. She couldn't keep a cry
from escaping her lips.

"Over there!" The voice was too close.

She stumbled around the picnic table and ran again,
reaching the deep shadow of the building next door.
Behind her, she could hear what sounded like an entire
army literally beating the bushes for her.

Her heart slammed into her chest, making the pain
of her limbs throb in time to its beat. She forced herself
to slow down, knowing that she was more likely to
escape without sudden movements that would draw
attention to her whereabouts.

As she approached the corner of the building, she
heard a sound a little ways behind her and froze. She
turned carefully around, needing to see whatever
seemed to be on her trail.

Arms, out of nowhere, snaked around her nude
body, one pinioning her arms to her sides, the other one
covering her mouth with a hand. She was pulled around
the corner of the building, out of sight of her pursuers.

Hot breath blew over her ear, sending chills
throughout her body. "Screams are best reserved for
pleasure, Lady. Do you understand me?"

She nodded. His voice triggered memories in her—hot, sweaty memories of earlier, before the world went to hell. Her body responded, liquid heat centering in her abdomen. The ache in her joints turned hot. She leaned into his body, aware of the hard ridges of muscle pressed against her shoulder blades, her buttocks, and her thighs.

It was real, she realized. Ez'iri was right. The plasma unit malfunctioned, and for some reason, this warrior chose to stand in for his plasma-generated double. Panic about the deception piled on top of the panic about Kenneth and his diabolical plotting, and the panic about the imminent future of human-Alcaini relations, tripping an internal trigger. It was all too much to be hysterical about. She straightened, deciding then and there that her panic button was officially out of order.

She was still a scientist, dammit. She sucked in a deep breath. In a bare whisper, she murmured, "I'll want to ask you a lot of questions later, but for now, we have to get out of here. The transfer station's useless."

"I have a craft, Lady," he breathed into her ear, sending heated chills dancing along her skin. "No Alcaini noble would claim his mate without a vessel."

Good thing she'd already reached her daily quota for panic. Hearing him claim her as a mate in the same breath as realizing he was real and not a simulation would have had her gibbering at his feet, otherwise. "I'll deal with the mate thing later," she muttered to herself. After she learned why Tai'en exercised the elaborate deception with the plasma generator.

He slid his hand down her arm to grasp her fingers.
Her body reacted to the inherent sensuality of Alcaini
movements. Her clinical detachment began to dissolve.
Wouldn't Kenneth be proud?

"Come, Lady. Let us be gone." Without much more
warning, he shot across the compound. Her arm nearly
came out of its socket at his speed. She ran to keep up,
her bare feet pounding on grass, then pavement. The
warm wind caressed her naked body and her breasts
bobbed painfully in counterpoint to the slam of her
soles on the ground.

Pebbles dug sharply into her feet, adding sharp
points of pain to the catalogue of aches already beating
at her senses. She couldn't keep a whimper from
escaping her lips.

At her noise, he turned and with one fluid motion,
scooped her up into his arms. The heat of his body, the
torment in hers, combined to shove her senses into
shutdown mode. *I just can't deal with this right now*,
she thought. *I don't care about anything, anymore.* She
let her mind go blank. Whatever was going to happen,
would happen.

* ~ *

She didn't know how long she stayed in the gray fog
of semi-consciousness, or what happened during her
stay in la-la-land. She came back to herself on a
reclining couch, similar to the medical bays on the
larger Alcaini ship. She sat up slowly, her eyes drawn
to the narrow, rectangular viewport across the room.

Outside of it, against a sparkling black background of stars, the African continent drifted sedately past.

I'm in space, she thought numbly. She rushed to the viewport, ignoring her aches and pains to press her nose against it, absorbed with the awesome view. When she'd been on the Alcaini main vessel, there hadn't been any viewports in the medical facility. She could have been in New Jersey for all it felt like space.

Lost in contemplating the spinning Earth below her, she didn't hear him approach. His hands landed on her shoulders, causing her to jump. Instant heat seeped into her body from his hands. She couldn't help but lean into him.

"The vessel meets with your approval?" he asked.

She turned to look at him, disbelief making her squeak. "My approval?"

"It's tradition," he said, as if that explained it all. "An Alcaini bride receives from each of her mates a vessel for her pleasure. My kinswoman has half a dozen."

"But I—we're not—I didn't even realize you were real!" she finished on a note of frustration.

His hands soothed her skin, running lightly up and down her back. Belatedly, she remembered she was naked. "Do you think it would have changed what happened between us?"

"Hell, yes! I asked Ez'iri for a simulation. A *simulation*! Not a real man." She turned in his arms to look at him. "Why did you come to me instead of letting the unit generate a simulation?"

His golden Alcaini eyes, gleaming like fireflies in
the subdued light, gave away little. "You spoke so
powerfully to my kinswoman. I knew we would have
the same mind about mating."

"And what mind is that?"

"We mate only with each other."

She curled her lip. "You'll find that many humans
hold that mind. I'm nothing special in that sense."

"I have felt your body come to satisfaction with
mine. Do you tell me that every human woman would
do the same, feel the same?"

His body, his hands, his words were making her
melt. "I—Maybe." She closed her eyes. "But what
about your children?" She had to be insane—here was a
man pledging fidelity and monogamy to her and only
her, and she was actively giving him an out through
reproduction? Hell, why not—with the day she'd had.
"Alcaini and humans can't breed offspring."

His sensual lips twisted wryly. "With the myriad
problems my people have in getting heirs, having a
mate of a different species is only one of a host of
elements conspiring against us." He put his hands on
her shoulders and turned her to face the viewport. "It's
safe for us to leave orbit now." He reached above her
head to a small panel she hadn't noticed before. A few
taps from his fingers, and the craft accelerated
gracefully. Another tap, and the panels on either side of
the viewport opened soundlessly, exposing a star-
riddled night to her. The earth hung like a huge marble
on diamond-studded black velvet.

Her mouth opened in a round O. She couldn't tear her eyes away from the astounding view.

"Come, Lady, let us find pleasure again."

The view before her and the male behind her combined to form a potent, heady combination. Wordlessly, she spread her legs, arching her back to allow him easier access. She was already slick from his whispered words and unconscious caresses, which now grew more purposeful. Long strokes down either side of her spine, around her flanks, along the curves of her hips to dance along the top of her copper curls.

The merest touch of his fingers sent sensations skirling through her at light speed. Somehow, during the night's events, she'd become even more sensitive, more sensual. The play of his hands over her body opened her from inside out and she groaned, her need sudden and fierce.

He parted her folds, dipping into her pooled heat. Her knees went as liquid as her cunt and she dropped, still seduced by the amazing view before her. Beyond the great marble of the planet, the vast emptiness of space coaxed an answering echo of the need that begged to be filled inside her.

She felt him against her inner thigh, silken heat pulsing against her sensitive flesh. *Two.* The thought thrilled through her.

His fingers filled her suddenly, and she bucked backwards, a moan escaping her lips. "You are so ready for me," he murmured, leaning down to flick his forked tongue over the mark he'd left earlier. The motion was purely possessive, and she ought to at least make a token protest.

The sound died in her throat as he drew her back against him. He took his time letting his hands roam around her body, pausing to cup her breasts and lift them, as if offering them to the stars in the endless night before them. Her nipples pebbled.

He splayed her legs. In the faint reflection of the window, she could see her own pale form, the thatch of curls at the apex of her thighs a dark shadow blending in with outer space. His fingers made a ruddy slash through the patch of starlight as they found and teased her clit. In some surreal way, she could have been fucking the stars.

But this wasn't surreal. It was quite real, and so was he. Her body stilled, her blood throbbing in pulses that centered on her clit and her nipples.

"What keeps you from pleasure?"

The fear of vulnerability gripped her. She searched for the words. "My—desires—have been used to betray me."

He brought his other hand up to cup her jaw. "Do not fear, Rayne'iri," he murmured. "Your desires are my desires as well. To betray you would be to betray myself, and bring me dishonor."

Just like that, huh? She reminded herself that there was no reason not to trust him. So far the only people who'd truly betrayed her were her fellow humans. She relaxed against him, slowly thrusting against his fingers once again.

Her juices trickled out of her pussy, sending a feminine musk into the air. He coaxed more moisture forth, and trailed his fingers down to her ass. She felt her rear muscles flex and open. "Fill me, please," she begged, her head dropping back to rest between the bone ridges protruding from his chest.

"Lean forward, just a bit," he said, "And we will find our pleasure together."

She obeyed and he slid his hands under her hips, lifting her. She felt the slick slide of his aft cock between the lips of her pussy, while his forecock probed her rear passage. She tilted her hips to allow him better access and he filled her with a single thrust. Pleasure spiraled out from her center to her extremities.

The awkward sitting position kept her immobile but for the small range of motion her hips could give her. He began to thrust inside of her and gripped her hips tightly when she wiggled. "None of that," he murmured.

"None of—what?" she gasped out as waves of sensation lapped at her.

"Keep your body still, insatiable one." His tone held a trace of amusement.

"Still?" She tried to buck her hips against him. "You'll drive me insane!"

"Let the pleasure overcome you," he said. He put action to his words, thrusting into her with more force.

Yet every time she arched her hips back to meet him, he would stop. "Please!" she said, her voice harsh. "Do I have to beg?"

"No, Rayne'iri, you simply have to hold still."

In the end, and after a few chastising pauses from him, she did. Her stillness was rewarded by harder and faster thrusts from him. She caught his reflection in the glass as his skin lightened to lavender. His features were taut, his lips drawn back over sharp Alcaini teeth, his eyes gleaming yellow points boring into hers in reflection.

She reached behind her, stroking her hands up and down his corded thighs, reached farther back to feel where they joined. She used her fingers to brush against his balls and was rewarded with a low growl from him.

Suddenly, she found herself face-down, flat on the floor, his body covering hers. "Rayne'iri," he ground out, "Forgive me, my lady. You have coaxed the control from me. I cannot fight my mating urge any longer."

"At last," she murmured. His teeth grazed the back of her neck as he pounded into her. Pleasure shot through her in waves that crested upon each other as her body stretched to accommodate him. The speed and power of his thrusts kept her from moving herself and all she could do was lie there and drown in the sensation and the stars.

Her orgasm tore through her, ripping a scream from her throat. He found his completion on the heels of her scream as her pussy flooded and throbbed around him. Her yawning hunger had once again been fed.

He collapsed on top of her, his weight pressing her into the floor.

"You've a wound on your neck," he said, a short while later. "One that I did not give you."

With a shock, the passionate haze around her mind cleared. Memory of Kenneth's words—a biological delivery system—returned and brought terror in its wake. "Oh God," she moaned, pressing her knuckles to her teeth. Her whole body started to shake. How could she have been so stupid, so careless, so completely clueless? "Oh, Tai'en," she said miserably. "I think I've just killed you."

Chapter Five

He rolled off her. Breath returned to her lungs with a whoosh, but her body remained leaden. Replete satisfaction warred with pounding fear.

Fear that he didn't seem to feel. "I believe you may have, Insatiable One."

She winced. A pet name! She'd just killed him and he gave her a pet name. "Please, don't. I'm serious. I think I might have killed you." She explained about the microbes Kenneth had injected into her and about her delivery system theories. "Whatever they slipped me must have suppressed my inhibitions and good sense, thereby ensuring the microbes in my bodily fluids would transmit to you."

His dark red lips pursed into a frown. "We will talk later about your refusal to acknowledge your own desires. But this disease you speak of must be addressed."

She rolled over onto her back to glare at him. "I've already ditched a boyfriend for mixing psychology and sex in bed with me. Let's break the cycle, huh?"

"Your use of idiom confuses me, Lady."

"Your use of psychology annoys me," she retorted. "And your calm about all this drives me positively crazy."

"Be at ease, Rayne'iri. We will be at the home vessel shortly, with access to their full medical facility."

"No! We can't go near there! I have no idea if the microbes can be transmitted through the air or not."

He shrugged. "The technology exists to quarantine us safely."

She remembered the plasma-generated sims of Ez'iri and the other Alcaini doctors who first examined her. "I hope your faith in it is warranted," she muttered.

He turned to his side and trailed one finger over her stomach in a light geometric pattern. "Abandon your worry, Rayne'iri. We will solve the problem when the time is right."

How could he be so philosophical about this? "Did I mention that I die, too? I'm not ready to meet my great reward yet."

He smiled. Alcaini smiles all looked slightly feral to her, but this one seemed positively wolfish. "My Lady, only a human would hesitate to receive reward."

She rolled her eyes. "Idiom again." Exasperation colored her tone. "Great reward is an euphemism for death. Dying. The big dirt nap." While she launched into an unsolicited mini-course on human perspectives of the afterlife—or lack thereof, he rose from her side and crossed the room to another discreet panel built into the wall.

Feeling somewhat bereft of his presence, she trailed off, content to simply watch his movements as he pulled out a graceful crystal bottle and tumblers. He poured something fizzy and dark gray out of the bottle into the cups and handed her one.

She peered into it. Little bits of matter swirled around the bubbles. "It looks like an activated charcoal cocktail," she said. "If you're thinking to pump my stomach, the microbes were injected into my bloodstream."

"You talk too much, 'iri," he said. "It is a type of wine. Fermented fruit."

She frowned. "It looks like you drink it with a fork. What the hell? I'm in space, I'm fucking a real alien, and I'm a human biological weapon of mass destruction. Why not a drunk one?" She took a long pull.

The wine was surprisingly sweet without being cloying. She drained her glass and held it out for more.

He obliged. "In noble company, this wine is sipped. It takes seventy of your years to render a single pressing."

She nearly spit out her mouthful. Thankfully, she restrained herself. Seventy-year old hooch on any planet had to be expensive. "Do you have any water? I find I'm terribly thirsty. And Lord knows I wouldn't want to waste this."

He went to what she began to refer to as the "mini-bar" and pulled out another decanter, this one filled with dark purple liquid. "Flower juice," he said before she even had to ask. "It's a little more refreshing than water. On board a vessel this small, the fact that water is reclaimed is quite…obvious."

She wrinkled her nose. Given the obvious places from which water would be reconstituted, she could well understand why it wasn't the first choice of beverage for sentient beings. The flower water hit the spot for her, and she felt no guilt in holding out her glass for more.

Besides replenishing sorely-needed fluids to her system, the flower juice had a heady scent that reminded her of the soothing aromatherapy bath oil that she adored. When she'd drunk enough to ease the perpetual thirst that plagued her, she leaned back on the cushioned couch and closed her eyes. "Are you positive this juice doesn't have narcotic properties?"

The cushions shifted as he joined her on the couch. "I'm certain. However, it is rumored to have aphrodisiac properties." His smile was wicked.

"That explains why I'm feeling so randy, when I should be worried about the fact that I'm a walking time bomb." She shifted to look at him directly. "Why aren't you worried? At this very moment, you might be dying because of whatever Kenneth injected into me."

He shrugged. "Will worry change the circumstances?" He leaned in and kissed her, his tongue flicking against hers, his body pressing hers into the cushions.

Her own body instantly responded, but she didn't feel the frenzy she did before their first coupling on the vessel. This time, she wanted to explore. "I still don't understand how you can be so philosophical about it."

He stroked her flank. "Your skin is so different. Fascinating and obscure." He cupped her breast, tipping his hand this way and that. Her nipple stiffened to attention, sending a stab of longing to her center.

She looked down at his hand moving over her flesh. The crimson ruddiness took on a pattern of light and dark hues, almost like the rosettes on a panther's pelt. The darker hues took on a bluish cast. "You're getting aroused again."

"Should I not? I am with the mate for whom I have waited many long years."

His words were pure fantasy—what woman wouldn't dream of hearing them?

But what woman could really believe them? Outside of the sensual, private world that was this pleasure craft, she might bring about the destruction of an entire race, one of who shirked his biological duty to reproduce by declaring his fidelity to her.

And those reasons seemed to be the very reasons she should take a page from his book. Outside—they weren't outside, though. They were here, suspended among the stars, and alone. Why not indulge in a little fantasy. If she was fated to die in a few hours or a few days' time, then God knew she deserved a little of her own.

She ran her fingers over the bone ridges on his torso. He drew in a sharp breath and let his head drop back. One of his cocks twitched against her thigh, rousing from its sated slumber to stand at attention for her.

She smiled wryly at the purple turn her thoughts had taken. They matched the shade his skin was beginning to color, "Do you like that?"

He opened one yellow eye. In response, he tweaked her nipple and trailed a finger down to slide into her curls. "Alcaini spurs are sensory centers. Direct stimulation is…"

She leaned down and flicked her tongue over a prominent spur just above his pectoral muscle. He hissed sharply and grabbed her shoulders. "You—how goes the idiom—make a game of fire?"

"Play with fire," she replied. "And I intend to keep on doing it." She shrugged his hold from her and bent her head again.

He responded by flicking the finger at the apex of her thighs. He petted her folds, circling her clitoris with maddeningly slow strokes. She sighed in response.

"You are a puzzle," he murmured, eyes intent on her face. "I have only your eyes and the expression on your face to tell me if I please you."

She smiled faintly. "That's pretty much all you get with a human," she said. Then a wicked idea occurred to her. "Of course, there's my voice, too. I could tell you how good your finger feels touching me." She felt deliciously brazen for having come up with the idea.

His dark lips curved upwards, and his skin lightened another hue towards lavender. "This is a good practice," he said. "Speak more of your desires."

"Mmm," she said. His finger stilled. "Keep touching me."

"How shall I touch you?"

"Touch me like you were just now doing."

He resumed his patient stroking. "Tell me what else pleases you."

"Your tongue," she said boldly.

He stuck it out for her. "What is it about my tongue that pleases you?" The forked tips curled. She knew from study that he could scent the air like a reptile, but the trait was largely vestigial, left over from the early evolution of his people. But the usefulness of a forked, sensitive tongue wasn't lost on her.

"I have imagined your tongue…" she faltered.

"What, 'iri? What have you imagined about my tongue?" He flicked it over her lips, featherlight touches that seemed to carry static electricity.

It was a lot easier for her to keep silent and act wanton than to actually talk about it. "I have imagined you…" she looked down, "—licking…"

He leaned in close, his breath tickling her ear, "Licking where, Rayne'iri? Where do I lick you?"

Heat suffused her body. She flushed from her belly up to her face, where she knew her face must have lit up like a Roman candle.

"Ah, now I see you color."

"That's embarrassment," she said. "Redheads tend to show it more readily than anyone else."

"Why are you embarrassed? Do the acts of pleasure bring you shame?"

He was genuinely puzzled. She owed him at least an explanation. "I'm not comfortable with telling my lovers what I want so—explicitly."

"I am of the mind that this is a good thing," he said. "Comfort is not the objective of pleasure. Now tell me again, 'iri." His tone changed, became harsher. "Where do I lick you?"

Excitement and trepidation mingled within her. She licked dry lips, wishing for more of that flower juice. "Umm, I've imagined—what it would feel like to—to have you l-lick me...where your finger is." She chickened out at the last minute.

He removed said finger. She made a small sound of protest.

"I don't understand you, Lady. Perhaps it is the language."

She blew out a frustrated sigh. *Language, my left tit*, she thought. He knew damn well where she wanted him to put his tongue. "You're going to make me say it, aren't you?"

He showed teeth, his tongue flicking out to dance around the finger he'd taken from between her legs. The gesture called forth a hot stab of desire. He leaned over. Her skin heated at the smooth, almost cool slide of his tongue as he circled first one nipple, then the other. He laved a path down to her navel, then up again. Her mind focused, then centered on having that tongue right where she most wanted it. "I want," she gasped out, "I want your tongue—in my pussy." God, she hoped his vocabulary included the vernacular!

The last illusion that her behavior was un-premeditated dissolved as he forced her to meet his eyes. "As you desire, Rayne'iri. I will lick your pussy." He lowered his head.

Reassured that he wouldn't go searching for a cat, she let her own head tip back, anticipation rushing over her, waiting for the touch of his tongue on her most intimate flesh.

Although she prepared herself, when it finally came, the shock of it threw her. She knew her clit was sensitive, but the touch of his tongue sent an almost electric shock through her. She came off the cushions, nearly bending in half.

He slid one hand up to nestle between her breasts and, with the lightest of efforts from him, pushed her body back down and pinned her to the cushions. The only thing she could do was clutch at his arm as his tongue worked magic on her feminine flesh.

He circled her clit, his tongue dancing along her labial folds. She was acutely aware of the forked tip as it slithered on either side of her swollen bud. Who knew the two tines could move independently! And who'd have guessed it could feel so good?

Without warning, he plunged his tongue deep inside her dripping slit. His tongue tips began a whirring dance inside her, sending electric shocks shuddering through her.

His tongue thrust in and out of her, faster and faster. Her hips writhed as her body tightened. Waves of intense pleasure crashed over her repeatedly, racing her towards a wall of sensation. Before she could catch her breath, she came without warning, a long wail erupting from her throat as her pussy convulsed around his dancing tongue.

On the heels of orgasm came a crippling lassitude. Her limbs felt molten, heavy. All her energy was devoted to simply keeping her heart beating.

"Sleep, replete one," he murmured softly as he withdrew from her. "I will tend to the vessel."

Her eyelids fluttered closed, and she lost the battle for consciousness. Her last thought was that she ought to remind him they lived on borrowed time.

* ~ *

She awakened, for the second time in her life, in a sterile environment, a bright light shining in her eyes. Her body was held immobile on an Alcaini med couch. As far as she could tell, she was still naked. She screamed, a short, sharp cry, as something pierced her upper arm.

"Reflexes are excellent, "a wry voice echoed through the room. A pair of yellow Alcaini eyes appeared, along with the rest of Ez'iri's head, in her field of vision. The light dimmed back to the normal, subdued light of an Alcaini medical bay.

"Ez'iri," she mumbled.

"Ez'iri sends her regrets," the Alcaini woman said. "Her kinsman has explained the situation. We thought it best to reinstate the plasma simulators."

The field holding her immobile released. She drew in a deep breath and sat up. On the far wall, a large

window separated her from a trio of Alcaini. Ez'iri
waved at her. She waved back. The plasma-sim Ez'iri
said, "Do you remember Physicians Belis'iri and Irek'iri
from your first visit?"

She nodded. Irek'iri's head spurs were prominent,
even for an Alcaini, resembling a crown sprouting from
her head. Belis'iri was more petite, delicate, yet her
keen intelligence had allowed her to be the first to find
common language between them. "I'm sorry we have to
meet again under such circumstances," she said to the
three behind the window. "Umm, Ez'iri…where is your
kinsman?" Their wisdom in quarantining her would be
lost if they let Tai'en run free around the ship,
secondarily infecting hither and yon.

Ez'iri's lips turned downward. "Your lover is in a
separate quarantine area, to prevent re-infection."

Rayne put her head down. Ez'iri hadn't wanted to
give her the plasma unit. If she'd listened to Ez'iri in the
first place, maybe she wouldn't be in this position now.

A plasma sim of Belis'iri materialized in the room
with her. Behind the window, the real Belis'iri was
busily dictating commands. She focused on the sim.

"Rayne'iri, please extend your arm that I may
sample your blood."

Rayne complied. "That sounds positively
vampiric." Belis'iri stuck a needle into her arm. Belis'iri
just looked at her, a puzzled expression on her face.
"Idiom again," she said lamely.

Both sims withdrew, and Irek'iri and Belis'iri left
the observation room. Rayne was left alone with her
friend. "Ez'iri, I'm sorry."

Ez'iri wouldn't meet her eyes. "I share your sorrow, my friend."

"If I'd have listened to you, maybe things would have been different."

"The fault lies with me. Had I not encouraged your friendship, you would not have requested something of me I could not resist."

"Hey, wait a minute." She hopped off the medi-couch and walked towards the window. She'd been all set to take the blame for their predicament, but Ez'iri went too far. "Don't you blame our friendship for this," she said, a sick feeling lodging in the pit of her stomach.

Ez'iri made to leave the room, still avoiding her eyes.

"Dammit, Ez'iri! Blame me all you want, but don't you regret our friendship!" With Ez'iri's departure, the plasma sim also vanished, leaving her alone.

She paced the quarantine room. "Ez'iri, come back here!" she called out. She knew her friend would still be observing. "I can help! I'm a scientist. I can analyze data. Something!"

No answer came. She explored the medi-couch's drawers and was rewarded with a sheet made of the semi-sheer, gossamer starlight fabric the Alcaini favored. She fashioned a sarong out of it and resumed her pacing.

She didn't know how much time she spent alone in the quarantine room. Around two hours after Ez'iri left her, she began to feel warm, then feverish. Judging by her heart rate and the hot, dry feeling of her skin, she guessed whatever she'd been injected with was beginning to take its toll on her system.

The coolness of the floor offered a little relief, and she lay down on it, spreading her body so that as much of her skin touched the cool surface as possible, and slept. Fever dreams kept her from getting deep sleep, so when Ez'iri returned, she was hot, groggy, and cranky.

She wiped gummy sleep from her eyes and warily watched her friend as she programmed a plasma unit.

"We need more of your blood."

"Ez'iri…"

"Please," Ez'iri said. "Our tests demonstrate illogical anomalies."

"Of course they do," Rayne said, disgruntled and grumpy. She folded her arms. "Ez'iri, I'm bored out of my skull in here, and I'm starting to feel sick. I may only have a few hours to live. Could you at least give me something to read?"

Ez'iri's gaze flickered up to her face and back down again. Her skin paled to a distressed yellow-green.

Rayne went to the window. "Look, I know you think our friendship is at fault for this, but I don't regret getting to know you one bit. You've shown me a little bit of what it's like to be an Alcaini, and if there's one lesson you've taught me, it's that the Alcaini don't give up easily. In some cases, humans can be just as stubborn."

Tears shimmered in her friend's eyes when she finally looked at Rayne. "Rayne'iri, you do not understand the consequences of your choice to mate with Tai'en."

Rayne looked down at her hands. "I do, my friend, believe me. But however much I regret it, there were two willing partners present at the time." And yes, she had been willing. "Is he—does he show any signs of infection?"

Ez'iri's eyes clouded and her skin deepened to a grieving orange-gold. Rayne's stomach hit the floor. "Oh, God, I've killed him, haven't I?"

She was unprepared for the rush of regret and grief at the loss of her lover. Had it taken such a short time for her heart to be seduced away from her by an exotic star-dream? Morbidly, she thought maybe it would be a good thing she didn't have much time left.

Stop being melodramatic, she ordered herself. "Ez'iri, I'm so sorry," she murmured, placing her hand on the glass in front of her friend.

Ez'iri placed her own hand on the other side. "Our hearts are breaking together," she said solemnly.

Rayne let the tears fall, taking little comfort in the moment of shared emotion that breached the barriers of species and galaxies.

"Tai'en will know no sons, will know no daughters."

Her heart really did split on hearing that. "Is there—will there be an autopsy?"

"Auto…"

"Autopsy," she said. What a time for the language barrier to rear its ugly head! "Examining of the body to determine cause of death."

Ez'iri frowned. "I doubt my kinsman would remain still long enough for that."

"Huh? But I thought…" *Hope springs eternal*, she thought wryly.

Ez'iri's skin ruddied again. "No, Rayne'iri. My kinsman is not dead. I grieve because he insists on seeing you, and will not comply with Physician Irek'iri's requests for testing until he does."

Her shoulders sagged in relief. "Oh, good heavens, is that all?" She wiped the tears away with the back of her hand.

"All?" Ez'iri asked in disbelief. "You ask if that is all, when Tai'en has slaughtered his hopes of siring children just as surely as if he had perished already?"

She remembered, with more than a little guilt, Tai'en's words about mating only with each other. It didn't occur to her at the time, but now she realized just what the implications were. They were extremely unlikely to have children. "But I thought that Tai'en's choice was a shame, rather than a sin. That it brought regret, but not dishonor."

Ez'iri looked intently at her. "His choice not to take a mate brought regret without dishonor. We at least entertained hope. Now he has changed that action. He has chosen a mate—deliberately chosen a mate—who cannot provide him with heirs. And since he will not accept multiple mates, he will not have offspring."

She looked at the floor. "I can't defend what I did, but I can't explain what he did."

Ez'iri snorted. "There is little to explain. I am loath to admit that our people have an attraction to other races. But it is uncommon for those of my family's status to pursue the mating urge outside of our own people."

"A little elitism of the nobility?" she asked wryly. "Isn't it usually the other way around—the nobility get to keep the exotic foreign sex slaves?"

"And waste the chance of conceiving a child on an Alcaini woman? Or deprive an Alcaini woman of the chance to mate and bear a child?" Ez'iri raised an eyebrow.

"What about those among you who already have children? Aren't you then free to pursue your desires with other races?"

Ez'iri shook her head. "It is too much of a double-standard. No, Tai'en has chosen and mated with you." She looked down. "No Alcaini woman can satisfy his desires after he has mated with an outworlder."

She couldn't help feeling just a tiny bit pleased at hearing that she'd spoiled him for any others. But that tiny bit of pleasure carried with it a huge suitcase full of guilt.

Ez'iri's yellow eyes once again bored into hers. "My kinsman must mate and produce heirs, Rayne'iri. Do you understand me?"

Rayne held her gaze for a long moment. In that moment, she knew what she had to do. Ever since she'd awakened that first time in the Alcaini quarantine room, she'd been a part of something bigger than herself and her own hungers. "I do, Ez'iri. I do."

She'd been prepared to live out her life with only a single, intense experience of fulfillment at the hands— and other parts—of an Alcaini plasma sim. For a brief time, she might have entertained the fantasy of having her Alcaini fantasy lover at her side for more than a single interlude, but all that would have changed even if she hadn't made the mistake of letting Kenneth into her quarters.

The plasma sim Ez'iri drew another sample of blood—at this rate, she'd be a pincushion within a day's time, if she lived that long. Her real counterpart said, "Tai'en comes to you shortly. He refuses to be denied."

The short time between Ez'iri's exit and Tai'en's entrance gave her little time to strategize. She knew what she had to do, yet she had no plan as to how to do it. His abrupt appearance in a hole in the wall that suddenly just wasn't there didn't help her composure, either.

"Rayne'iri." His low, purring voice went straight to her solar plexus. If anything, he drew her attention even more forcefully. Her eyes traveled greedily over his powerful form, a loincloth-like garment the only thing barring her view from absolutely everything.

"I hear you're giving your kinswoman fits." She stepped closer to him. *I shouldn't have done that*, she immediately realized. *It's just going to make things harder.*

"Her reasons for keeping us apart all this time are feeble."

"No they're not. They're quite biologically sound."

"Pah! They argue like philosophers rather than physicians." He put his hands on her shoulders. His eyes darkened to gold and deep colors flowed beneath the surface of his skin. "And they keep me from what I desire."

Her eyes fluttered closed as a stab of desire ran through her. God, when he talked like that, it was all she could do to keep from saying, "take me!" like some cheesy soap opera heroine. She settled for retaining a little dignity and merely whispering his name. Her own hands couldn't stay still and she ran them over his body, stopping to stroke the bone spurs she wanted to explore further.

I have to stop, she thought. "Tai'en," she said weakly. His arms came around her and dragged her to his chest. Her breasts pressed against his hard flesh, her nipples stiffening at the feel of skin on skin. His spurs were aligned just such to create little pressure points between the hollows of her ribs and just outside the areolas of her breasts.

His spurs narrowed to a vee, their points digging into her flesh with tiny pressures that pulled her awareness along behind them, to focus between her legs, where a dull heartbeat began to throb. She murmured his name again. "Stop this, please."

"No," he said. "I will not stop when we both desire it."

"I don't," she said. *Liar.*

He drew away. "Why do you deny us our desires?"

"My desire is to see you find a proper mate." It wasn't as bald-faced a lie as her first statement, but remained less than completely truthful. "My desire is to know your lineage will continue."

He put a hand on each of her breasts, massaging them. His palms scraped across her nipples. She moaned softly.

"Ez'iri has convinced you to reject me," he said. "Ez'iri does not know of which she speaks."

She let him continue touching her for a delicious moment, then stepped back. "Tai'en, you have to have children. Your people need all the offspring you can potentially get. And the only way to do that is with an Alcaini woman."

"A warrior knows when to fight and when the battle has been lost," he said harshly.

"Oh, stuff the melodrama, Confucius," she said, just as harshly. "If you think I'm selfish enough to put the entire Alcaini people at risk just for my pleasure, then why am I not roaming free around the ship, infecting everybody with whatever's inside me? This is your race's future, for crying out loud."

"My people have no future," he said brutally. "Every generation, no matter how frenzied the coupling, fewer and fewer of us can conceive. Within two generations, we will die out. There is nothing left for us but the present. Those who believe differently are fooling themselves, and my kinswoman knows it."

Two generations? She reeled. "But—in vitro fertilization. Fertility treatments." Ez'iri had the research!

His lips twisted. "Even the extinction of our people has not lifted that particular taboo from any but the most desperate."

"Then it's your duty to at least *try* to produce offspring! Nature has to find a way."

"I will not be denied, Rayne'iri." His tongue darted out to lick at her lips, lightning quick. The contact sent shivers along her spine and wetness between her thighs. Heat streaked through her.

To be desired that fiercely…

His eyes gleamed. "Your desire colors your skin, Lady," he said, referring to her blush. He trailed one finger down to her navel, circling it, sending flutters through her belly. "You still burn for me."

She realized he wasn't going to accept no for an answer. "I will not deny you what we both want," she said. "But is it fair to deny your kinfolk what they want, either?"

"My clan," he said, "do not make my decisions for me." He dipped a finger between her legs, stroking her slit. She was wet for him even now, when she was trying to send him off to another woman.

Ez'iri's voice filtered into the room. "Attend me in the purification room, kinsman Tai'en."

As Tai'en made to leave through the iris door across the room, Rayne reached for him. "Wait!"

He returned to her side and ran his fingers through her tangled hair. "Yes, 'iri?"

She looked up at him, drinking in the sight of him, from his crown spurs down past his brief clothing and powerfully muscled legs. His skin shimmered with subtle hue changes, letting her know that in spite of his becalmed stance, excitement simmered beneath his surface. Her own heart began to beat faster in response.

He bent his head and kissed her, long and deep. His tongue slid in between her lips, twining with hers, the forked tips tickling her. She melted into him for just a moment. "Go," she said after their mouths separated. "Before I tear your loincloth off right here."

Ez'iri's voice interrupted them. "Tai'en," she said, annoyance evident in her tone, "Must I remind you that the human woman is in quarantine for a reason?"

He shot his kinswoman a look, but made for the iris door. As it closed, she wished she had asked him to bring her something to do to keep her mind from nervously dwelling on the brevity of her future.

We're all living on borrowed time, she thought. She had who-knew-how-few hours left, the Alcaini had little time as well, relatively speaking. And if the Alcaini chose to retaliate against Kenneth's diabolically stupid idea, the human race might not have very much longer, either. Her only consolation was that at least she would be going out with—*ahem*—a bang.

Chapter Six

"Rayne'iri, I thank you for your efforts to turn my kinsman to the right path," Ez'iri said when she returned to the observation room.

Rayne drew her knees up to her chin and huddled in the middle of the medi couch. "Fat lot of good it did," she said. "And I can't say that I'm really disappointed. He's fascinating, and the way he touches me—no human male could even come close." She offered her friend a wry smile. "If it's any consolation, I'm not expected to live for very long. Maybe then Tai'en will settle down with a nice Alcaini girl." The clinical scientist in her accepted the fact with logical inevitability. Why then did she want to find this unrealized Alcaini and beat her senseless?

"Perhaps it is so. But your efforts are appreciated. The clan wishes to show you proper hospitality, inasmuch as we are able."

"Um. Great," she said. "Does that mean you'll find me something to do soon?"

Ez'iri smiled. "You must be feeling tired and unclean. That can be remedied immediately." She patted the glass once, then turned to leave as Irek'iri and Belis'iri entered the room. The Alcaini women exchanged looks and pressed hands against each other's. Moments later, their plasma generated sims materialized.

Rayne hopped off the couch and bowed to the Alcaini women, holding up her hands as she'd seen them do to each other.

Irek'iri's sim lifted the top off the medi-couch, revealing the hollow inside of the base. She pressed a key on the programming pad and the bed base began to fill with a rose-tinted liquid. "We cannot offer you luxurious private quarters in which to bathe, but we can offer you a bath."

She remembered her last bath and the disturbing vision she'd had. Then she remembered how long had it been since she'd had that bath. A heady aroma of exotic spicy floral teased her senses. She didn't have to be told twice to hop in. She sank into the water and closed her eyes, letting her body take a long moment to simply float, and listen to the women moving around. She heard them murmur to each other, and Ez'iri's voice joining the conversation, but their words were Alcaini, and she couldn't hear them clearly to attempt a translation.

"Are you comfortable?" Belis'iri's voice pulled her from the lazy haze of scented steam she'd been floating in. The Alcaini woman began to work the tangles out of her corkscrew curls.

She opened one eye. "Don't you have beauticians to do this?" she asked, as Irek'iri took one of her hands and massaged it. "Not that I'm not grateful, but you're Physicians. Giving me a bath is not the most effective use of your skills."

"We are also women, and Alcaini." Belis'iri's fingers raked gently along her scalp as she explained. "Neither of us has been so close to an outworlder before."

"That makes three of us," Rayne mumbled.

"And an outworlder who has mated with one of us is even more rare, Irek'iri said. "It makes me wish there was a Commun…"

"Hsst," Belis'iri interrupted. "The elders would be furious to hear you speak so."

Rayne opened the other eye in time to see Irek'iri's eyes flash. "The elders are quick to proclaim Communion abhorrent, but only so after they have experienced it," she said angrily. "In their youth, Communion was still an honor. Now suddenly it is forbidden? More likely they seek to deprive us of the joys they took for granted."

She looked from one woman to the other. "What is this Communion?"

"It is one of the oldest rites of our people," Irek'iri said. "When an Alcaini and an outworlder mate in the presence of the clan, the entire clan can experience the—secondhand effects."

"Secondhand effects?" The scientist in her begged to pursue this new and fascinating information. "You mean you get to watch?"

Belis'iri nodded. "According to what we've heard, the clan watches, and experiences."

She put a hand to her mouth, scandalized. "Kinky," she said around her fingers, a blush heating her cheeks.

Irek'iri winked at her. "The sharing of mating outside our people is a rare and celebrated honor. To witness it assuages our individual urges and helps us stand firm in our resolve to mate with each other and produce offspring. But our elders have determined that even the rare possibility of Communion is too much encouragement for us to mate outside our race. Hence, they have forbidden it," she finished somewhat bitterly.

"That's hardly fair, is it?" She thought of the information she had passed to Ez'iri on artificial insemination techniques among humans. Would it be too much to hope that Ez'iri would use the information, in spite of the ridiculous taboo?

Irek'iri's massage extended from her hand up her arm. The warm, scented water relaxed her muscles. "Mmm…I almost don't want to have to leave this tub."

Belis'iri began massaging her shoulders. The warmth from the tub and the smooth strokes of the two Physicians sent a spice-hazed languor seeping into her. "So I guess you can't tell me what goes on at one of these things. Other than the public sex, I mean."

Irek'iri shared a look with her compatriot. "Even if we could, we would not. It is not good manners to speak of such things." She dropped Rayne's arm and began working on her feet, moving up her calves in smooth, kneading strokes.

Belis'iri was a little more forthcoming.
"Communions happen so rarely, and so very few are
invited to one that it is better not to speak of them in the
presence of so many who will never have the honor of
attending one."

"Ah," she said softly. "There are politics involved.
Sex and politics seem universally entwined." She tried
to perk up enough to address her dissatisfaction, but her
body just wasn't willing to ascribe that much
importance to expressing her opinions on the subject.
"What a load of—whoa!" Now she did sit up, perky as
hell.

Belis'iri's hands closed over her bare breasts,
massaging and kneading, pausing to run her thumbs
over the peaks of Rayne's nipples, which stiffened to
attention, along with her suddenly clear mind.

"Hush," Irek'iri said. "What we do, we do to relax
you." The way her hands stroked up Rayne's thighs was
anything but relaxing. Her fingers brushed the coppery
thatch of hair protecting her most intimate flesh, and the
sensual fire that had never truly been banked from
Tai'en's touch flared to life and spread.

"I've—I've never been with a woman before," she
said haltingly. The thought hadn't even crossed her
mind. In fact, she'd very emphatically looked in the
other direction. If one cock wasn't enough, how could
no cocks do a damn thing for her?

"We have seen the way your females avoid contact
with each other, and we do not understand it." Irek'iri
spread her legs.

Fine trembling started in Rayne's thighs and seeped upwards. The feel of soft, feminine hands caressing her body, so different from a man's—any male's—was even more foreign to her than making love to an alien male. Yet, the taboo nature of it stirred an intense curiosity in her. She wanted to discover more—wanted to learn how the scene would play out, what emotions and sensations she would experience. "Is this…" Irek'iri's fingers parted her labial folds and she gasped. "Is this something all your females do?"

Belis'iri's tongue touched the sensitive skin behind her ear. "Yes," she hissed. "This is how we are close."

Her voice was raspy, and for some reason, Rayne thought of the snake in the Garden of Eden. *It's just the forked tongue*, she thought. "But don't your mates get—ooh—jealous?" Irek'iri's finger found her clit and stroked it long and deeply.

Irek'iri paused to look at her. "Why? It is not mating we do, merely pleasure."

"But it's s-se-sexual," she managed. Belis'iri's tongue had moved down to join her fingers in circling her nipples.

Irek'iri tossed an amused look over Rayne's head to Belis'iri. "No male would dare deny his female the comfort and closeness of her clan sisters."

"Even Tai'en?" she had to know.

Irek'iri's smile widened. "Who do you think chose us to attend you? Your mate wished you to have trusted attendants. Ez'iri herself would have been here as well, were she able."

In a bizarre way, his gesture was thoughtful, and seemed in line with what Irek'iri was telling her. She felt comfortable with Irek'iri and Belis'iri, as they'd been her physicians since her first encounter. *Now they're my lesbian lovers*, she thought wryly. For a very short to-do list of things before she died, she never imagined even putting this one on the bottom. *Stranger things have happened.* Well, no they hadn't. But what the hell.

Irek'iri's finger caressed her pussy lips until they swelled and opened, then slid her finger into her cunt. Rayne moaned softly. "God, that feels good," she murmured. Belis'iri licked and sucked at her nipples.

Once she'd accepted the experience, she couldn't simply lie back and be passive about it. She reached one languid hand out to Irek'iri's head and stroked her prominent crown spurs, remembering how Tai'en had enjoyed her tentative touches.

Irek'iri made a small sound and looked at her wonderingly. "You know of our spurs."

"Not much," she admitted. "But this isn't all one-way."

"Yes," Belis'iri said, "it is. Perhaps you will one day return our favor." Gently, but firmly, Belis'iri clamped her hands around Rayne's wrists and pulled them above her head.

She gasped as a shudder rippled through her. She was virtually helpless against the sensual onslaught of her attendants, and the feeling started a delicious quiver deep in her belly.

Irek'iri's finger slipped in and out of her pussy, one thumb caressing her clit. Rayne's hips twisted of their own accord.

"You are fascinating to view," Irek'iri said. "Your *iriwai* has but one receptacle." She touched her tongue to it, as if to explore, and Rayne came out of the water entirely, splashing spice-scented drops everywhere. Shudders of pleasure rippled through her and she spread her legs wider. That forked tongue would be her undoing.

She turned her head to one side, as if to escape the sensations, and met Belis'iri's yellow eyes. "It feels good, yes?" she asked.

Rayne nodded. "Oh, yes."

Belis'iri kissed her, her feminine lips soft as they pressed against Rayne's. Rayne was amazed at how delicate the kiss was, compared to the kiss of a man.

Between her legs, Irek'iri's tongue lapped at the well of her pussy, darting up to circle her clit. As if things couldn't get any more intense, the Alcaini woman sucked her clit between her lips, pulling and stretching the ultra-sensitized nubbin of flesh. Her finger stroked long and deep, finding a spot inside Rayne's vagina that sent her exploding in brittle shards of static electric light.

Her heart pounded and her blood roared in her ears. The rush of pleasure spiraled through her and out in a long moan that took her up, then returned her to her body, little licks of aftershock pleasure quivering through her as Irek'iri's tongue slowed its lapping.

Belis'iri lifted her head and released Rayne's hands, trailing her fingers lightly down the length of her arms in soothing, sensual strokes. She rose from the shallow bath and went to the same wall from which Tai'en had produced a communicator. The magic wall now opened a beverage panel similar to the one aboard Tai'en's personal craft.

"More flower water," she said delightedly. Then she saw the dark crystal bottle. "And hooch!"

She accepted a glass of the fermented stuff from Irek'iri. Belis'iri turned from the panel and presented her with a blue-colored puff of something. She looked at it questioningly.

"It is a delicacy," Belis'iri said. "Compatible with your digestive system and not detrimental to your nutritional requirements."

The carefully chosen words weren't lost on her. "Like chocolate is not actively detrimental to nutrition," she said, more to herself than to them. "Never mind. It'd take too long to explain." She took a tentative bite of the blue puff, all the while knowing that the word 'delicacy' in reference to food could just as easily refer to the sublimely disgusting as the sublimely delectable.

The blue puff turned out to be somewhere between the two extremes, sweet, but floury, like a dry sugared cake that had been left out for two days. Inside, a dark red, syrupy liquid oozed out around her teeth and tongue, cutting the sweet taste with a salty one. The effect was unusual, but not unpleasant, and reminded her of eating holiday rum balls.

"Eat," Irek'iri said. "You will require strength."

An absurd comment about qualifying for the Sex Olympics jumped onto her tongue. She bit it and drowned it in another bite of the syrup-cake. Irek'iri pressed a button and the water drained out of the tub. Warm air began to circulate in its place, drying her off, except for a fine sheen of scented oil that made her feel decadently slippery. She stepped out of the bath gingerly, testing her knees for strength in the liquid afterglow still sending occasional washes through her.

Satisfied that she wasn't going to collapse, she joined her friends around the tray of syrup-cakes near the magic wall. The odd taste combination was growing on her and she munched through a handful of the blue puffs in between sips of flower juice and fruit booze. The nagging thirst that plagued her ever since she'd first made love with Tai'en must have been a by-product of sex with Alcaini.

"Come, Rayne'iri." Belis'iri put the tray back into the magic wall. "Let us join the rest of our clan for a real meal."

Her stomach fluttered nervously. Belis'iri and Irek'iri stood by the wall and the iris door opened. They waited.

She didn't move. "Umm. Did you two forget that I'm in quarantine for a reason?"

"That reason no longer exists," Irek'iri said. "Come."

She frowned. "What do you mean, it no longer exists?"

Ez'iri appeared in the doorway. Rayne gasped. "Ez'iri, are you crazy? You're exposing yourself!" Even though she knew it was a futile gesture, she covered her mouth with her hand.

Ez'iri smiled and held up a data stick. "Come, my friend, and understand. Your health has been given back to you."

Rayne blinked. Ez'iri activated the data stick. "We have confirmed several times. The microbes present in your body when you first boarded the main vessel decreased in number with each new blood draw, until we confirmed twice that they are no longer present in your system."

"You mean, I fought off the infection?" she asked in disbelief.

"If you like. You are no longer a danger to anyone."

Rayne stared hard at the information projected on the tiny screen of the data stick. Sure enough, the numbers didn't lie. She breathed a heavy sigh. "So Tai'en is healthy, too?"

"The plan of your esteemed colleagues has failed." Ez'iri's tone was dry, even for an Alcaini.

"Thank heavens for that." She raised her eyebrows. "You're not planning to obliterate my entire race for that, are you?"

Ez'iri showed teeth. "Suitable justice will be exacted on the guilty."

Rayne gulped. "Please don't blow up my planet," she said in a small voice.

"We do not indulge in the habit of eradicating the species with whom we meet. Even if our relations are unfriendly. Your Kenneth will be dealt with—later.

Now is a time for celebration." She held up a spun-starlight tunic-looking thing.

For the first time, she noticed her friend's dress had changed. Gone was the utilitarian, many-pocketed kimono in favor of a loose shift, beneath which the flickering hues of her skin glowed. Rayne took the proffered garment and slipped it over her head. The fabric caressed her oiled body and she wondered if the awareness—the heightened sense of just being alive—came from the garment and the massage, or the knowledge that she wouldn't self-destruct in the very near future.

"Come. All of you."

Irek'iri and Belis'iri stepped out of the room.

Rayne blinked. "You two—aren't plasma sims, are you?"

They smiled. "We replaced our sims while you were in the bath," Irek'iri said.

"I told you, Alcaini carry a deep fascination for outworlders," Ez'iri threw her a look.

Rayne stepped through the iris door. "I'm starting to think you people find it funny to switch with plasma sims at the last minute." For the second time now, she'd ended up having sex with real Alcaini, rather than safe plasma sims. She ought to be outraged, but she couldn't find the indignation. Both times, she'd been intensely, immensely satisfied, so who was she to complain?

A smile twitched at her lips, as she comprehended the absurd logic behind that conclusion. The smile faded when another iris door opened, revealing Tai'en. Her breath hitched in her throat.

Chapter Seven

Tai'en's presence filled the doorway. "I trust your bath proved…pleasurable?"

Her tongue suddenly stuck to the roof of her mouth. Beside her, Irek'iri and Belis'iri suppressed aqua-humored smirks. "F-fine," she stammered. What was it about him that made her brain melt?

"Leave us," he said quietly.

Irek'iri shot him a look. "I assume there will be a council meeting after the feast?" she asked, an edge to her voice.

Tai'en nodded. "It is so."

Irek'iri did not reply, but worry pushed the hue of her skin towards the green and Rayne wondered if she had anything to do with Irek'iri's green or the troubled expression on Ez'iri's face.

The women filed out the iris door and left her alone with him. She looked at the floor. It was amazing how free she'd felt when she thought she didn't have long to live. Now that the heaviness of impending doom was off her shoulders, it was a lot easier to notice the weight of the consequences of her actions.

"Tai'en," she asked, forcing her voice above a whisper. "What's going to happen to me?"

He looked down at her. "You are mine," he said, as if that explained everything.

She loved the shivers that went through her when she heard that possessive note in his voice, but it didn't answer her question, nor did it drive away the stomach-churning fear of the future. "And," she prompted.

"And we will return to the homeworld soon. I have a fine house with many gardens to please your senses." In sharp contrast to the hardened soldier she knew him to be, he spoke of his home with almost bashful pride. "The breezes blow sweet scents through the corridors, and even at the heat of the day my house is a cool embrace. I have loyal servants to see to your needs and comforts, and high walls to assure your safety."

"My safety?" She had little idea what the Alcaini homeworld looked like, or what their politics were, and she wondered if that lack of knowledge might prove hazardous to her health.

"Mates of other races are highly controversial among my people. Some will go to great lengths to acquire one. Others will go to great lengths to eliminate them."

"You mean my life's in danger?" The sudden obscurity of her future—now that she had one—slowly froze her from inside out.

"No!" His features turned feral. "I would never permit harm to befall you."

"How could you stop it?" She raised an eyebrow. "Never mind—that was a rhetorical question. What do the other outworlders do, then?"

"Do?" He looked puzzled. "They serve their mates."

"That's all?" Visions of herself in a ridiculous harem outfit feeding him peeled grapes brought a smile to her lips. And a clench to her stomach. "I have a brain," she said, a little crossly.

"Surely you do," he agreed affably.

She leveled a look at him. "I mean, I'm good for more than just sex. Where do outworlders work on the homeworld?"

"Outworlders do not have functional positions on the homeworld."

Then I'm not going, she thought, dread creeping through her. She'd quite honestly rather be dead than useless.

"Why not?"

He shook his head. "Non-Alcaini do not have independent status in our society. The Alcaini mate sees to all their needs, and any status they hold comes from the Alcaini to which they are mated. If a male of higher rank than I were to succeed in taking you from me, he would be permitted to claim you as his mate."

She'd been sipping her flower juice. She choked on the sweet brew. "That's—that's barbaric!" she sputtered, wiping away the juice from her chin with the back of one hand. "Isn't there a way to apply for citizenship or something?"

He shook his head. "It protects the sanctity of Alcaini to Alcaini relations and keeps our homeworld in our own control. We are a diminishing people. Aliens would quickly take over our world were we to allow them rights such as citizenship."

"And what if they overwhelm you with sheer numbers?"

"They may win our world, but it will be a blasted and burnt out shell, rather than the civilized paradise it is now. But make no mistakes, 'iri," he said, his voice darkening, "We hold what we have claimed. None shall take you but I."

That's not what I'm worried about, she thought miserably.

He turned to her and took the cup from her hand. "Rayne'iri." He looked intently into her eyes. Her breath hitched in her throat at the glow in his yellow eyes. "Many of us spend little time on the homeworld. Life on the clanships is not luxurious, but it is more relaxed. As my mate, you will have a place beside me, and on the clanship, your intellect will bring me much honor."

"Oh," was all she could manage. Warmth pooled in little corners of her heart. While she had been a keen student or a valuable employee, no one had ever spoken of her cerebral tendencies as honorable.

He cupped her chin and kissed her gently, almost chastely, except for the fact that nothing he did could ever be construed as completely without sensuality. "Come. Let us attend the feast."

She followed him to a large hall in the center of the ship. "Wow," she murmured, as he led her over to a low table where Ez'iri and a few other familiar faces knelt. Everyone on the ship had to be in attendance here. Hundreds of Alcaini eyes fixed on her as she sank to her knees next to Tai'en.

The low tables were set with wide, shallow bowls at each place, and large platters of whatever food was to be served at one end of each table. Diners passed their bowls down to the end and back to be served. The tables radiated out from an open space in the center where a cluster of lights emitted a soft, ruddy glow. Around the edge of the room, dozens of large drums stood like sentinels.

She watched the others eat carefully, intently, before touching anything on her own plate. She was starving, but there was a lot of food back on her home planet she wouldn't eat—she wasn't at all sure about any of this. So she took tiny bites and made a lot of conversation while she waited to determine if she'd have any immediate reactions. "I sincerely hope," she said to Ez'iri, "that you didn't get all fancy on my account."

Ez'iri patted her shoulder. "My friend, this is but an intimate, informal gathering aboard an exploratory clanship. Back home, attendance at one of our moderate feasts can number in the thousands." Periodically, a handful of feastgoers would rise from their table, go to the drums, and thump out riffs that seemed to have more meaning than dinner music.

"That's a hell of a party to plan." She passed her bowl down for the next course and was delighted to see it return full of the blue puffs she'd had with Irek'iri and Belis'iri. "What's the significance of the lights in the center?" She wished she'd paid more attention to Reese's cultural work. He would have loved to see this, she thought with a pang of homesickness.

"On the homeworld, that is where the sacred fire burns."

"Oh," she murmured. Nothing in any of Reese's reports had mentioned anything about religion. During the project, the Alcaini had been rather close-mouthed about their homeworld. She didn't blame them. She'd be just as closemouthed when meeting another species for the first time.

Amidst all the sex and telepathy and biology, she'd forgotten about Kenneth and his cronies' diabolically stupid plan. God, but it was a dead shame that the complexities of this culture would now be lost forever to planet Earth because of a small minority of xenophobic idiots.

She looked down at a half-eaten blue puff. She might be a guest of honor at this feast, but she was still a guest. Would she ever truly be one of them? Not likely. Would she ever understand them? Maybe. She could spend a lifetime trying.

Around her, talk turned to the attempt on her life. Without a doubt, the human-Alcaini scientific exchange had crumbled. Out of the dozen team members plus the scant handful of military and government officials who knew about the existence of extraterrestrial life, someone had already perceived the Alcaini as a threat and had taken steps to neutralize them at the expense of human life—*her* human life, to be specific.

One older Alcaini—although, she couldn't really call him old by any stretch as his cranial bone spurs were barely two inches long—pounded his fist on the table. "This betrayal of trust cannot go unanswered. Our honor is at stake!"

A woman spoke. "Do you think we have not begun to prepare to avenge this insult?" More goblet-banging ensued. A handful of young-looking males rose and pounded a martial-sounding beat on the drums.

She wouldn't mind a little vengeance herself, especially on Kenneth. She had a mental picture of herself returning to Earth to personally deliver the message that their biological weapon had failed. Kenneth would be livid, his professional ego insulted by her very existence.

Of course, her revenge wouldn't come without a price. Kenneth had said his partners were in the military. He might be a wuss, but she'd bet money that his cronies wouldn't shy away from attempting to nuke them out of the solar system, and she couldn't even begin to list all the ways that could go wrong.

Across from her, several young Alcaini males caressed their ceremonial staves, as if they longed for functional ones. Everyone on board took this insult personally. She realized with a start that there were easily several hundred people just as eager for revenge as she was. She could comprehend one mad scientist demanding vengeance, but several hundred aliens ready to enthusiastically carry out that vengeance?

Another elder lifted his ceremonial staff in the air. "Payment in flesh for the insult!" His cry was met with cheers. Rayne began to get nervous.

A few women across the room began an ululating war cry. "Let the rivers run with their blood!" Soon the Alcaini were thumping staves, goblets, bowls, and drums. Beside her, Tai'en thumped his goblet against the table.

"Wait!" she said. The banging rhythms continued. "Stop!" She put a full lungful of air behind the second call. Around her, the people at her table stopped banging to listen.

She flushed a deep, hot red as the attention of a dozen frenzied Alcaini—several of whom she'd slept with, although right now that seemed more of a disadvantage than anything else—focused on her. "Please! These crimes were committed only by a few people! My planet is full of innocent folk who bear you no ill will." *And who don't even know about you.*

"Justice must be exacted," came the reply from one woman she didn't know.

"I agree," she shot back. "But only on the guilty parties. Not on innocent bystanders. It's not how we do things."

The woman's lip curled. "We have seen the way humans dispense justice. It can be bought with a sack of credits waved in the right direction."

She would have to bring that up, wouldn't she? "Bloodshed doesn't change the past," she countered.

The man who first spoke raised his voice again. "It is our way, outworlder. You will not interfere!" She remembered Tai'en's remark that outworlders had no rights on the homeworld.

"It's my planet!" She rose to her feet.

To either side of her, Tai'en and Ez'iri pushed her back down. "Not now," Ez'iri murmured in her ear.

"Rayne'iri, we are not an unnecessarily violent people," Tai'en said.

Bullshit, she wanted to say. What else did he call it in the middle of a blood frenzy, then?

"There are other ways," Ez'iri said.

Around them, the call for blood and revenge thundered from the throats of hundreds of Alcaini. *Kenneth, you stupid fuck, what have you gotten us all into*? But then again, she wasn't entirely blameless either, thanks to her libido. "I'm sorry." she rose again. "I can't stay here."

They accompanied her out of the room, leaving the drums and shouting behind. Immediately, she turned to Ez'iri. "You can't let them blow up my planet!"

Ez'iri stroked her upper arms. "Rayne'iri, my people are not given to unnecessary violence. But we are, nonetheless, honorable. Were my clan to let this insult go unpunished, we could no longer show our faces on the homeworld. Our entire families would be forever branded with the mark of shame."

She looked away from her Alcaini friend's yellow distress. Strong emotions had never been her forte. She didn't understand them—either in herself or in other people—and preferred to work with clinical facts. "How much blood will it take, then?"

"It is not a question of bloodshed, my passionate one," Tai'en said. "We are also a disciplined people. Do you not trust me?" He put his hands on her shoulders and turned her to face him.

She had no choice but to look into his gleaming yellow eyes.

"Food and pleasure will make the whole ship sleep well this cycle," he said. "The feast serves as an outlet for their expression."

It wasn't foolproof assurance, but she wanted to believe it, so she latched on to it and nodded, dropping her gaze from his. Tai'en took her hand and led her back to his quarters.

She forgot her fears momentarily at her first sight of personal living space on board an Alcaini ship.

His sleeping couch lurked in one corner. Blankets of a sumptuous fabric were folded neatly on its lower edge. A single container, utilitarian in design, hulked at the foot of the couch.

It was the walls that softened the place. Intricately designed with raised reliefs, they depicted geometric patterns that moved fluidly between multi-colored insets of some sort of stone that glowed from within, like alabaster when held up to a light.

The telltale pattern of seams in a smooth portion of the wall next to the sleeping couch indicated the presence of one of those magic consoles. She put her own hand on the panel and true to form, a panel popped out with the ubiquitous decanter of flower juice. Someday, she had to climb into the back of one of these and discover if an army of gnomes ran from room to room, setting out decanters and glasses like some sort of secret, demented kitchen staff. She poured two glasses of the flower juice. Her hands shook slightly as she handed him his glass.

Besides the small comforts of the magic panel, his storage trunk, and the sleeping couch, every other part of the sinuously-decorated wall, from the iris door, all the way around and back again, was lined with weapons.

Staves ranging from short batons to ceiling-scraping ceremonial spears with flags tied to the tops stood to attention with military precision. Her eyes widened at the sight of an intricately carved staff with a hollow end. Darkened blast marks stained the mouth of the hollow. *Just like the one they first pointed at me*, she thought. She'd suspected they were some sort of blaster, and she'd been right. Good thing nobody had been trigger happy during that initial encounter. Blades worthy of Mel Gibson's Braveheart performance wedged between the staves, their edges glowing with a silvery light. She reached out to touch one.

His hand clamped down on hers. "That is an atomic microblade. The cutting edge begins far sooner than you can see." He tossed his cup towards a curved blade. Flower juice splashed out of it. The arc of liquid split in two around the glowing edge. The cup separated into pieces before her eyes, without even touching the blade's visible edge. Two halves clattered to the floor.

She picked one up. The cut edge was hot to the touch and she dropped it again. "Damn," she muttered, bending down to examine it. Though hot, the edge showed no signs of breakage, no sharp edges. It was as if the other half of the glass had never existed. It would cut through flesh and bone like half-melted butter.

His smile was chilly. "These are but the weapons I travel with."

Say what you will about them, she thought, *they certainly have a bloodthirsty streak*. If each of them were as well armed as Tai'en, what they lacked in numbers, they could make up in technology.

A cold lump formed in the pit of her stomach. The Alcaini could very easily decimate everyone in the research compound—which included a hell of a lot of innocent people, as well as the handful of guilty ones. And they had reason to—that handful of guilty had tried to kill them all in the first ever instance of human intergalactic mugging. Kill the Alcaini aboard the ship. Then take their technology using the transfer stations.

The Alcaini had shown her honor and given her pleasure, while her people had betrayed their trust. The Alcaini would take revenge, and humanity would make them pay for it. There was a reason why her logical mind was so misunderstood among her peers.

Someone had to stop it.

Both sides had to be stopped, and fast. Heaven help them all if shock troops from Earth showed up here to meet atomic blades and blaster staves.

She looked up at Tai'en's face. In spite of his alienness—his reptilian eyes and tongue, his vividly shifting skin tone, the bone spurs jutting proudly from his flesh, something she could only define as humanity hung about him, in stark relief to the differences between them. She could easily spend a lifetime discovering all the nuances that lurked behind the differences and similarities. An interspecies war wouldn't allow her that kind of chance, not with one of its warriors.

She traced little circles with her fingers around his pectoral bone spurs. "Why me?" she asked suddenly, desperately. "I know you said you heard my conversation with Ez'iri, but what made you choose me?"

His head tipped back as he silently enjoyed her caresses for a moment. His skin tone began to shift and change, slipping from bright apple red and burgundy to deep purple and black. Even though she'd grown used to seeing Alcaini mood changes, it still gave her a start. With the deep coloring, a frighteningly intense fire flickered in his eyes. A thrill of primitive fear ran through her.

"I first believed it was Ez'iri who could not control her fascination with humans. I—how do you say it— hacked into her program for the plasma emitter and discovered that her human friend held as much fascination for me as I hold for her."

She blushed, remembering her request to have Ez'iri program a "passing resemblance" to her kinsman into the simulator. She'd gotten a hell of a lot more than a passing resemblance.

He reached for and captured a lock of her wildly curly hair. "Bipedal species are common in our experience. Women as beautiful as K'tenq sunsets, as sensual as the healing waters of Yephon, and as spirited as wild bikkik. None have compelled me as you have. I cannot explain it, and I do not question it. It simply is."

She didn't have an answer to that. His words didn't answer her question in the least, but they moved her. She couldn't help but lift her hand to his face and caress his crown spurs. She stood on tiptoe and kissed him, twining her tongue around his forked one.

A low hiss came from back in his throat. "Lady..."

"Shh," she said, filled with a deep, preverbal knowledge of what to do next. She pushed him down on the sleeping couch and began a path with her tongue, licking each of his bone spurs from torso to abdomen.

His cocks sprang to attention, twin staves standing proudly from the softly furred nest of his crotch. While her fingers caressed his lowest pair of abdominal bone spurs, she opened her mouth and closed her lips around the plump, satiny head of his forecock.

Warm, musky scent of male rose to meet her. She used her tongue to trace little patterns along his rigid flesh, eliciting a groan from him. With her free hand, she cupped one set of his balls, running her nails lightly along the sensitive sacs.

His hands fisted in her hair, drawing her locks up to spread over his stomach. She moved her mouth to his aft shaft and left off fondling his bone spurs to milk his forecock while she sucked the aft. His hips began an involuntary thrust in time with her strokes.

There were so many different things to try with him, and he welcomed them with low growls and groans. The cocks beneath her hands and mouth rippled with colors from lilac to indigo. His rosettes pulsed in time with his thrusts. She explored the length and breadth of him to her heart's content, noting the subtle ridges spiraling along the length of his aft cock, and the angular bend of the fore.

Prompted by a memory of their first time together, when she was emboldened by the thought that he was only a simulation, she brought her hands together, so that the tips of his two cocks touched and fastened her mouth around them.

Her instincts were on the mark. He bucked off the couch, his long, low growl echoing through the room. She used her hands to stroke his shafts while her lips and tongue played with the sensitive heads. Through it all, she reveled in the feeling of power she received from giving him pleasure, and when he came, she milked him eagerly of every last sticky drop, her heart beating in time with his pulsing shudders.

Later, after he dragged her up the length of his body to nestle in the circle of his arms, she watched him at rest. The hard lines of a soldier softened at rest, the angles of his face relaxed. His lips curved upwards in a slight, mysterious smile, and he looked so—human. Just as vulnerable as she was.

God, he was going to hate her when he woke up to find her gone.

Whether in the lab or outside of it, Rayne always insisted on cleaning up her own messes. She considered

herself partly responsible for bringing at least some of
the variables in this explosive cocktail together—the
logical thing to do would be to isolate the volatile
components. A couple of light-years between them
ought to do the trick.

All she had to do was destroy the transfer station on
Earth. The Alcaini couldn't invade her planet, and
Kenneth's military goons couldn't invade the Alcaini
ship. It didn't matter that she had no plan, and couldn't
take any weapons or even take clothing with her into
the transfer station.

I'm really starting to think like an Alcaini, she
thought grimly.

Once she was sure Tai'en was asleep, she slipped
out of his quarters and headed for the medical lab at a
run. Ez'iri and Irek'iri both looked up as the iris door
swirled open.

"Don't mind me," Rayne said as she shrugged out of
her kimono and leapt naked onto the transfer station.
Before either Alcaini could reach her, she slapped her
hand on the activation pad and nausea overtook her,
Ez'iri's worried yellow-orange skin tone the last thing
she saw.

* ~ *

Much as she'd expected, there was a welcoming
committee waiting for her. Maybe not her, personally,
but two armed guards stood next to the transfer pad,
weapons aimed at her. She put her hands up. "As you
can see, gentlemen, I'm not armed," she said dryly.

One guard took her by the arm. The other stepped back, a horrified look on his face. "Flynn, get back! You remember what Taggart said about her."

Flynn's hand on her arm flexed, then loosened. Beneath the stolid soldier's impassivity, she saw alarm flash in his eyes. The subtle scent of fear reached her nostrils. How she knew it was fear, she couldn't say, but she knew.

As far as they know, I'm still a walking bug bomb. Good. She drew in a deep breath and coughed, hamming it up for good measure. Both Flynn and his compatriot flinched.

The main door opened, letting in a sliver of light and the man she hoped would come to see her. She folded her arms and smiled. "Well, hello Kenneth."

His eyes widened. She arched an eyebrow. "What, no kiss?"

"You—you should be dead!" He looked decidedly peaked, even in the dim light.

Cold air caressed her bare skin as the air cleaners kicked on. She felt it dance over the individual hairs on her arms as she savored the priceless look on Kenneth's face. She offered him a saccharine smile. "Did I forget to do that? Gee, sorry, Ken. Maybe I should write it on my hand or something."

He fished in his pocket and pulled out a mask, fumbling in his haste to put it over his nose and mouth. Above the sterile mask, his eyes held panic that she could taste on the back of her tongue, metallic and tangy, like limejuice in tequila.

She made to move off the pad and both soldiers immediately pointed their guns at her. She stepped back. "Easy boys. I have some unfinished business with Dr. Mengele, here, then I'll be out of your hair."

One rational part of her marveled at the cool bravado she exhibited in the face of two armed men and a psycho ex-boyfriend who all wanted her dead. Especially since she had no plan as to how she was going to destroy the transfer station, and no way to escape, either out to the world or back to the Alcaini ship. Her actions probably took stupid to a whole new level, but so far, it seemed to be working, so she went with it.

To her left, the gel-like substance that powered the transfer pad glowed softly. Green-gold streaks swirled through it, pulsing with the power generated by the chemical reaction of the elements. One good thwack and the protective container holding the chemicals would shatter, rendering the pad inoperable. The only kink in her plan was that the protective container was very, very protective. It would take more than a simple thwack to break it. The best she could hope for was to crack the container and hope the power failsafe would kick in and shut down the transfer pad.

Still, she had to try. Kenneth motioned to the two guards. "Take her."

Flynn and his buddy didn't move.

"Oh, go on," Kenneth snapped. The guards turned to look skeptically at him. She used the opportunity to edge closer to the power cells. "The virus is only transferable through bodily fluids—not simple touch."

She saw the subtle shift of the soldiers' bodies what seemed like minutes before they began to turn. She had to make her move now or never. She balled up her fist and threw all her weight into the punch, hoping against hope that something besides her fingers would break.

The shock traveled up her arm. Her knuckles sent streaks of pain lancing through her, and shards of crystalline silicate shattered in all directions with a loud report that blew her completely off the transport pad and into the guards, tumbling them all over in a heap. Her head cracked against the concrete, sending stars swimming through her vision, but she could still see green ooze dripping from the shattered power cell. *Holy crap, I did it!* was her last thought as the stars took over her vision.

Chapter Eight

I really need to stop losing consciousness so often. I miss a hell of a lot while I'm out cold. Like how she woke up on a table in her own bio-lab in the research compound—and where the hell the restraints came from.

She heard the aluminum clatter of sterilized instruments and followed the sound to where Kenneth, hands shaking and muttering to himself, lined them up on a tray.

"Blood and saliva show no trace of the virus, therefore I must test deeper. Deep tissue samples, full gynecological workup, spinal fluid—one of those has got to turn up answers."

Full gynecological workup? A spinal tap. "Kenneth, what in the name of nine hells are you doing?"

He jumped, spilling a pair of scalpels haphazardly across the tray. "What are you doing awake? The dose I gave you should have kept you out for hours yet."

"Story of my life," she muttered, more to herself than to him. "But if you think you're getting anywhere near me with any of those things."

"I don't see how you can stop me, Rayne. I must have my answers." His calm tone was betrayed by his still shaking hands and the stink of fear that practically oozed out of him.

"You think you'll get them by cutting me up?" He couldn't be that stupid. "You're a psychologist, not a surgeon."

"I had training in gross anatomy early in my career. One doesn't need to be a surgeon to know how to dissect a specimen."

"Dissect—Kenneth you've seriously lost it." She kept a tight lid on the panic that wanted to bubble over inside her. He might not be that stupid, but he could be that crazy.

"The delivery system was foolproof," he said. "The microbe was so viral that no human immune system could develop a resistance to it."

"Well I did, I guess."

"Not during testing."

Now he wasn't even making sense. "Huh?"

"Your DNA was used as a test sample when we selected you as the delivery system. Your DNA disintegrated under the attack of the microbe, exactly as every other human test sample did. The Alcaini test samples, of course, took a little longer to react, but they were still no match for the virus. No." He shook his head and ran an agitated hand through his hair.

"Something changed." He pointed his finger at her. "You changed."

He'd infected her right after she'd come back from her first, intensely pleasurable simulation—or rather, the first time she and Tai'en had mated. Regret washed through her when she realized that her reckless dive into the transfer station would likely mean she'd never see him or any of the other Alcaini again.

She hoped that with the destruction of the transfer station they would have the sense to get the hell out of the solar system before somebody on earth did something really stupid, like lob a nuke at them. If it came to that, it would serve them all right to have the entire planet bombed.

But back to the situation at hand. "Kenneth, you're insane. You don't have the training to figure out why your weapon didn't work. And might I add, I'm rather glad it did fail."

"I'm not insane Rayne, I'm scared."

"At least you're honest."

"I won't live as a slave under an alien rule."

"You really are insane. What under the sun makes you think the Alcaini want to take over the world? They already have a handful of their own." With her arms and legs bound, her only weapon was her voice. What she wouldn't give for one of those atomic blades from Tai'en's room.

"They represent a threat to us. They have more advanced technology—they could defeat and enslave us at any time."

"And the fact that they've never even hinted at the desire plays no part in this?"

"It's a pre-emptive strike. We must maintain our security."

"At the expense of making them even more likely to want to blow us out of the solar system!" She yanked at the restraints.

"What do you care, anyway? They're not like us."

"They're still my friends," she said hotly. "And decent people. They don't deserve our hate."

"They're not people!" He narrowed his eyes. "I can't expect you to understand. You've been unnaturally obsessed with them from the start."

She shook her head. This wasn't the Kenneth she'd dated. This wasn't even the Kenneth that used her private life as a psychological profile for money and glory. Only a few short days ago, he'd been rhapsodizing about the sublimeness of Alcaini mating practices, insisting on calling them 'lovemaking techniques.' "What happened to you, Kenneth?"

He pulled a marker from the tray of instruments and uncapped it. "My eyes were opened." He drew a line from her navel to her sternum.

Panic hit her in earnest now. "You're sick, Kenneth. You've been misled!"

"General Druring has the highest credentials. He's been studying the Alcaini as long as we have."

"General Druring?" Who the hell was he? "The only military contact we have on the team is Colonel Paulsen and he only checks in once a month to see how much money we need. This is private-sector research."

"My dear Rayne, who do you think is funding it—privately, of course." Kenneth finished drawing on her skin and turned back to the table.

The military connection explained the biological weapons angle, and Kenneth's own ego explained why he absolutely had to know why the virus didn't take. The disconnect was between Kenneth and the military. He was about as private-sector as anyone could get. What could convince him to climb into bed with the military?

The answer to that would have to wait. He turned back to her with a scalpel in one hand, snapping a rubber glove on the other.

She tossed her head and twisted at the restraints, fear sending bone-numbing cold through her. "Kenneth, stop!" She heaved her shoulders up off the table and felt the sockets in her arms scream for mercy.

He pushed her back down. His expression grew confused for a moment. "Hello, what's this?" His latex-covered fingers brushed over her collarbone, along the bruise where Tai'en had bitten her. "It looks like an Alcaini mating bite." His tone dropped to a whisper. His eyes were wide as they met hers. "You've had sex with one of them, haven't you?"

She stopped her struggling for a moment as Kenneth's eyes bored into hers. The disgusted expression on his face cut her, and pulled out of her all the disgrace she hadn't yet felt over what she had done to and with her alien mates. "You always could make me ashamed of myself," she said quietly.

It hurt most because she'd been secretly wondering if her desire for Tai'en was healthy. Kenneth hadn't been wrong back when he'd concluded that humans and Alcaini *could* mate, but *should* they. Ez'iri, in spite of her friendship, disapproved of Tai'en's choice to mate with an outworlder. She should have run far and fast when she found out her simulation really wasn't.

Why hadn't she? Where had her logic gone?

Tai'en was unlike any man she'd ever known—not just because he was an alien. The clinical detachment that made up most, if not all, of her personality, abandoned her when it came to dealings with him. He pulled her out of her comfort zone and made her more than she was without his presence.

"You *have* been fucking an alien," he repeated. The way he said it, softly, as if revulsion robbed him of the breath to speak, burned through her shame and left a smoldering anger in its wake.

What made what she was doing any sicker than what he was doing? At least she wasn't using unsuspecting members of her own species to start an interspecies war with another race that harbored no aggression towards them. She narrowed her eyes. And at least she never dissected anything that wasn't already dead.

Her eyes followed the scalpel he held and she knew he was growing impatient. "Yes," she said. "I've been fucking an alien, and you know what? It's incredible. You were right, you know."

The hand with the scalpel relaxed slightly. "I was? About what?"

She latched onto the reprieve. "The mating practices of Alcaini. They really *are* lovemaking techniques. Did you know that they can telepathically share their sexual experiences?"

"Indeed?"

She pounced on his reluctant curiosity and nodded her head. "Alcaini males," she lowered her voice, "*hunt* their mates. Like prey." She didn't know if it was exactly true, but as long as she kept Kenneth's attention, who cared?

"How barbaric," he said.

"Very barbaric," she replied. "They fight each other over mates." As long as Kenneth was listening, he wasn't cutting. "It's fascinating," she said. "While I was on board the Alcaini ship, I saw two men fight to the death, because one man brushed a woman's arm at a feast."

"*No.*"

Well, no, not really. In fact, not at all, but she wasn't about to tell him that. Instead, she nodded again. He had his fears already—trying to downplay them hadn't worked in her favor, but pumping them up just might do the trick. "They're very possessive of their mates." Kenneth carried the typical intellectual distaste for physical altercation and she played upon it. "Especially alien females."

"And you've become their whore," he said disgustedly.

Damn! She pushed him too far. Hell—he'd always been a better shrink. "Maybe I have," she said, abandoning the pretense of being calm. Was it her imagination, or did the restraints feel a touch looser?

He pressed the scalpel into her flesh. A thin line of burning pain shot through her as blood welled in the slice left by the blade.

"I'd rather be their whore than your lab rat!" She twisted her body away from the knife. Hot pressure enveloped the raw skin of her wrists and hands and suddenly gave way with an audible snap. Her hand was free!

She brought it down on his shoulder. It was an awkward strike, not designed for power, but it made him stagger nonetheless. "How did you—shit!" He swore and clamped his hand around her bruised wrist. His other hand still held the knife and it moved closer to her skin again.

She forced it free with less effort than she thought she'd need, screaming every curse word she could think of at him. Sweat seeped into the cut beneath her breasts and stung.

"Give up, Rayne. I'm stronger and I have backup." He leaned over and slammed a red panic button on the wall above her head that she hadn't noticed before. An alarm klaxon sounded, nearly splitting her eardrums. Out in the hallway, she heard the sound of many footsteps.

This is it, she thought. *The ride is over*. At the risk of seeming melodramatic, she sure as hell hoped her sacrifice was worth it for the Alcaini. If she lived long enough to miss Tai'en, it would be half a bad miracle— bad because she lived long enough, miracle because missing him would mean the Alcaini ship was out of reach of General Druring and whoever else had crazy latent xenophobia.

The footsteps grew louder. Many voices shouted outside the room—what, she didn't know, but she imagined they were military. She kept pummeling at Kenneth, instinct keeping her fighting for life.

Then the lights went out.

* ~ *

In the darkness, which she realized wasn't complete dark—she could still see everything, just through a dark green filter—the building got quiet. As one, she and Kenneth froze, locked in their awkward version of a life-and-death fight. She heard an occasional shout, and the soft rustling of something above her head. Across the room, the latch on the door rattled.

"Who's there?" His voice held a high-pitched edge of panic. "Flynn? Parezzi? Is that you?"

In the bottle-green world, she gasped for breath and searched for an indication of her impending fate. The doorway was a slice of black in a forest-green world, but above her, another slice of black appeared. A dozen bright yellow pinpoints hovered, one pair of them detaching from the group, dropping silently to the ground to prowl stealthily towards the table. She didn't need a lamp to figure out whom they belonged to.

"My God. They've invaded," Kenneth said in a breathless whisper full of terror.

She met Tai'en's battle-furious eyes. "Hello, Lover," she said. *He's going to strangle me*, she thought. The murderous look on his face told her as much.

Kenneth began to shout, fear-filled cries for help. Tai'en's fist shot out, almost a blur, and connected with his jaw. He dropped like a rock.

"Thank you," she said. Tension wound tightly in her limbs.

He reached for her remaining restraints and snapped them one by one. "You will follow Pryt'en to the vessel," he said. "You will obey his orders. You will not move unless and until he orders you to do so. If you disobey his orders, I will stuff you in a storage container and sit on you all the way back to the main vessel. Do I make myself clear?"

I've never seen an Alcaini this pissed. She nodded nervously and sat up slowly. It dawned on her that there was an awful lot about the Alcaini that remained a mystery to her.

Outside, she could hear shouts and an occasional hollow-sounding foop, as if a projectile had been launched from a hollow tube of some sort. Her eyes settled on the staves of the assembled Alcaini soldiers. "Tai'en, how many troops did you bring?" Screams and shouts were getting closer now. She felt sick when she thought about the people who were dying right now.

"Enough," he said.

She put a hand on his arm. "Please," she said, her throat choking with fear, "Don't do this. Don't fight a war over this."

His eyes were hard. Cold.

Alien.

"Go," he said.

Pryt'en, apparently the youngest of the troops, as his cranial spurs were little more than buds, moved up beside her. She glanced at him. He didn't look happy to be playing escort. *Good,* she thought. *I'm not in the mood to be escorted.*

She folded her arms. "Nuh-uh." She didn't want him to see her quaking in her nonexistent boots.

"I have not the time for this, woman," he said harshly.

She swallowed. The gentle lover she'd known, full of daring and desire and passions that ran deep, had another side. She'd left him sleeping, vulnerable. He was awake now, and girded in full armor. "I won't let you leave my planet a smoking crater."

He slammed the butt of his staff into the cement floor. Cracks webbed out from the impact and shards of concrete skittered across the floor. "It is not your place to dispense justice."

"I think it is." In spite of the deep cut beneath her breasts, her lack of clothing, and the pain in her wrist where she'd pulled free of the restraint, the worst pain wasn't the physical, it was the sick fear at seeing a different side of Tai'en.

"Pryt'en," he said. It was all he needed to say. The young soldier slid one arm around her and hefted her effortlessly over his shoulder.

She pummeled his back, for all the good that did. "Put me down!" She wished she knew enough Alcaini to call him an ass.

He carried her across the quad to the darkness of a large copse of trees near the building that housed the transfer station. The Alcaini vessel was camouflaged, and she couldn't even see it until Pryt'en put his palm against it and a crack of light appeared. The young warrior deposited her unceremoniously onto the floor of the craft and left, sealing the door behind him.

She spent the interminable wait alternately fuming and fearful, agitatedly pacing the confines of the utilitarian craft. With only fear and anger to amuse her, she grew quickly bored, and filled with the insatiable need to know what was going on outside. She located the magic panel and explored it more fully. In addition to the mini-bar, she found a control panel that sprouted a data terminal. The touch-screen displayed Alcaini characters, but many of them looked familiar from her research. Most of the entries were in red, with a few glowing white or yellow. She moved her hand to select one of the white ones, but something stopped her. Some feeling, an instinct, told her that white was bad. White meant danger. She selected a red menu choice instead.

The lights in the room brightened. She squinted and hit the choice again. The lights returned to normal. A few trial-and-error selections later rewarded her when a panel on the far wall flared to life. She settled herself on one of the reclining couches lining the walls. Even the Alcaini military traveled in style, she thought inanely, as she looked at the scene on the screen.

She could see the area outside the ship. Pryt'en stood stiffly, his body radiating deep green anger. Off in the distance, she could see much of the rest of the compound. It looked peaceful. Asleep.

She'd expected, like she'd said, a smoking crater. At least some fires. The blaster staffs wielded by Tai'en's troops weren't just for looking at. The quiet tableau was the last thing she expected.

The fear and the anger gave up fighting within her, abandoning her to uncertainty, which, she realized, was far worse. The military didn't trust the Alcaini. They took an aggressive stance against them that provoked retaliation. It was safe to say that humans and Alcaini were officially at war now.

A group of figures came into view, moving closely together with stealthy precision.

The door began to open. She clasped her hands tightly together to stop the shaking. Sour nerves bubbled in the pit of her stomach. If this vessel left earth with her on it, she knew there was no going back. She rose to face her fate on her feet.

Unreasoning panic seized her limbs when he entered the craft. His troops followed behind him, two of them bearing a large bundle, which they dropped onto the nearest couch to the door. She recognized the bundle as a person. Kenneth, to be specific, she realized as one of them removed the hood to allow him to breathe.

"*Hoomain-an'en engah a'uda wui ak,*" one of the soldiers said.

The others made surprised noises. "*A'uda wui ak? Jii-shao,*" another said, laughing.

"*Gin jii-shao. A'uda wui ak*," Tai'en said, as if that settled it.

The soldiers continued their conversation, their tone shifting from amazement to mockery to puzzlement. Laughter punctuated their conversation.

She didn't get every single word, and the nuances of grammar were lost on her, but she rolled her eyes nonetheless. The soldiers were making jokes about Kenneth's single, lone penis.

Men, she thought disgustedly.

Tai'en smiled at a few of the comments, but held himself a little aloof. She couldn't help but admire the air of leadership that hung about him, even if that leadership might result in her head getting cut off or something even more grisly.

His attention turned to her. *On second thought, I'll take that beheading. It'll be quick and painless, at least.*

The nerves souring her stomach exploded. Unable to hold herself upright anymore, she sank to her knees, fear and panic robbing her of strength.

Tai'en showed little emotion. The thought of begging for her life entered her head, but she'd never been very good with words. "Thank you," she said shakily, her eyes sliding to the viewscreen. "Thank you for not blowing up my planet."

His eyes flickered, but his tone held no warmth. "You owe me a debt."

She nodded. "I know."

"One which will not be easy for you to pay."

A fatalistic doom settled over her. She didn't have that kind of luck. "I'll do whatever it takes."

"How Alcaini of you."

* ~ *

The return to the mother ship was a change for her. For once, she was awake to see the graceful dance of shuttle and ship as they docked. The soldiers prodded a bound Kenneth through the airlock, where another squad took custody of him and disappeared down a hallway. She waited, tension stringing every one of her muscles taut. This whole adventure, no matter how diverse the situations in which she found herself, held the same common theme. "What now?" she asked Tai'en quietly.

Aboard the shuttle, she had several hours to contemplate her fate. She grieved for Planet Earth, relieved the Alcaini hadn't let loose on it, but regretful that she would never see her home planet again. The missiles that had chased them out of the atmosphere assured that there would be no more peaceful exchanges of knowledge. On the lighter side, she didn't have to apply for unemployment.

On the other hand, she wouldn't be able to collect her last paycheck. Or any of her clothes—not that she seemed to need them; she spent more time naked around the Alcaini than she ever had in her life. Or any of the knickknacks she'd collected, or the books in her library, or the library books she'd forgotten to return, or—dear heaven—chocolate.

By the time the shuttle docked at the mother ship, she swung back around to the positive. She was embarking on a great adventure that would hopefully last a long time from now, and not involve any jail cells or any more biological weapons.

Tai'en pushed her towards Pryt'en. *Him again.* "Go with Pryt'en," he said to her. "We will settle our quarrel soon enough."

Oh, good. More time to fret and worry. She spotted Ez'iri in the crowd. "Ez'iri," she said, waving her hand.

Her friend pushed through the line of military types and joined her. "You have been injured," she said. "Come to the medical bay and we will put you back together."

She looked down at the cut beneath her breasts. She'd almost forgotten about it, the burning subsiding to a dull sting that didn't merit any attention. It must not have been as deep as it felt. She made to follow Ez'iri, but Pryt'en held her arm.

Her friend looked at the guard. "Tai'en was most unhappy to discover you had abandoned him."

"I didn't abandon him! I just—I was trying to help."

Ez'iri's smile was sad. "Males do not think as we do, Rayne'iri. I understand that is true on your world also."

She rolled her eyes. "They get over it eventually," she said.

"You must make things right," Ez'iri said. "Alcaini do not let things right themselves."

Of course not, she thought miserably. That would be way too easy.

"I will come to Tai'en's quarters to tend your wounds."

Pryt'en dumped her into Tai'en's quarters and left her. She wandered around alone for a few minutes, helping herself to flower juice and wishing it was that charcoal-colored hooch. The door opened and Ez'iri walked in, carrying a small pouch.

"Thank you for coming," she said. She wanted to hug her friend, but instead, clasped her hands in front of her.

Ez'iri smiled. "You fear my kinsman, do you not?"

She nodded. "He's not happy with me. I truly didn't mean any insult to him. But I couldn't let innocent people die in a battle instigated by a few misguided idiots, when I had the means to stop it." She twisted her clasped hands as Ez'iri opened her medical pouch and pulled out a single, milky crystal.

"My people are more aware than you think of the value of a single life. Many of our soldiers are not yet fathers—we would be foolish to waste their lives on unnecessary slaughter." Ez'iri began to roll the crystal between her palms. Her motions gathered speed and the crystal began to pulse with a faint glow.

"Exactly! And there are a lot of humans down there who had no part of the plan. They were like me—curious, interested, and excited about meeting our very first alien species." She looked down at the floor.

Ez'iri's hands appeared in her field of vision. The crystal glowed with a pinkish light that dimmed as her friend held the stone nearer to her wound. Neither woman spoke as the crystal did its work, its force field pulling at her wound, knitting the edges together until only a thin pink line remained.

She looked up at Ez'iri with wonder. "I've never seen you use something like that before. It's amazing."

"We were forbidden to show it to the human team. The crystals come from a specific mine on a single planet. Their export is tightly controlled, and their properties are not fully understood, even by us."

"But the practical applications in the medical field are astounding."

Ez'iri offered a humorless smile. "The crystals' ability to heal is only surpassed by their ability to harm."

"It figures." Nature in Her infinite wisdom, and all that. "Good thing we didn't know about them, then. I'm sure General Druring would have wanted to get his hands on them." She traced her scar with a fingertip, feeling the pink, new skin gingerly. Heat radiated from it. "I take it I'm being shown this because I'm not going back to Earth."

Ez'iri shook her head. "By now, we are far out of your solar system." She began to work on her wrists, running the crystal over the swollen bruises and scrapes.

A pang of loss twisted inside her. She was really gone for good, now. "What will happen to me?"

"That is up to Tai'en. He has claimed you as his mate. As aliens have few rights in our culture, a sponsoring Alcaini has first determination of an outworlder's fate."

Tai'en had already told her of the need for Alcaini primacy on their homeworld. She understood it, but she didn't have to like it. At that time, she still held out some little hope that she still had options. Her options, however, seemed to have dwindled down to one. The person most responsible for her future fate was also the one who was angriest with her right now. Not a good combination. "Ez'iri," she said, "Tai'en holds my fate in his hands. He's not happy with me right now."

Her friend caressed the crystal in her hands, an unconscious gesture that nevertheless drew Rayne's eyes, the glow from the crystal tracing patterns in the air and flickering between Ez'iri's fingers. After a minute, Ez'iri spoke. "You have challenged Tai'en's ability to keep his family together."

She blinked. "I'm his family?" She'd never been part of a family before. At an early age, she'd entered a live-in program for highly intelligent children sponsored by a science foundation. She hadn't really missed the single, elderly great-aunt who was her only relative and she didn't think her aunt missed her, either.

Ez'iri nodded. "He has claimed you as mate. You are part of his household."

"So how do I make up for this challenge? I really didn't mean to insult him, you know."

"Nevertheless, the challenge still exists. He must reassert his dominance."

"And that means what?"

"The challenger must display submission. That means you."

"And what, exactly is a submissive display?"

Ez'iri reached into her pouch and brought out a thick coil of leather lacing. "Kneel," she said.

Rayne swallowed. "You want to tie me up?"

"How else do you propose to display your complete trust and loyalty to your mate?"

A nice flower basket? An abject apology? Something that *didn't* involve being bound?

Ez'iri took her hands and pulled them behind her back. "Worry not, my friend. The strongest of women can find pleasure in the discovery of a new dynamic."

The bonds were light, but strong. The hide felt cool and supple against her skin, an almost soothing counterpoint to the panic that shook her from inside out. Ez'iri wound the laces from her arms, bound behind her at the elbow, over her shoulders to criss-cross between her breasts. She wound the laces around her waist once, then put the ends between Rayne's knees. "Lift up," she said. Rayne rose on her knees. Ez'iri drew the laces between her legs and bound her ankles.

She looked down. "I feel trussed up like a turkey."

"Ah, but to our eyes, you look like a female willing to honor her mate." Ez'iri followed the laces with her fingers down between her legs.

"What are you…" she gasped as her friend's fingers swirled between her outer labia.

"There," Ez'iri said. "Now you are ready."

The laces nestled, cool and buttery soft, between her labia, on either side of her clit. When she shifted, the laces dragged over her sensitive inner lips. "Oh," she said, startled at the sensation.

She glanced down again. Sure, she could see Ez'iri's point. If only she could school her attitude to go with the picture of submission. As she regarded her crisscrossed breasts, she noticed the skin on her scar changing from pink to a pale yellow. "Ez'iri?" she said, alarm in her voice. The scar went from warm to cold.

Ez'iri bent to examine the scar more closely. "Curious. Very curious indeed."

"It feels cold." As they both watched, the yellow deepened to orange.

"Do you feel ill at all?"

She did an internal check. "No. I feel fine. A little tired, a lot nervous about what Tai'en's going to do to me when he gets here, but nothing out of the ordinary." And, she thought, a little turned on by those laces. But she wasn't ready to admit that to her friend yet. A radical thought tickled the back of her mind. Insane, impossible, illogical. She shivered.

"This will bear more study," Ez'iri said. "The crystals have never been used to heal humans before, however they have never faulted us on any other alien races." Her friend glanced up. "If you begin to feel unusual, speak immediately."

"Define unusual," she said dryly. Just then, the iris door swirled open, revealing a Tai'en with a vexed expression on his face. His eyes widened when he caught sight of her, packaged neatly on his floor.

"Ez'iri," she said, fear knotting her belly. She couldn't stop herself from tugging at her bonds. "I'm starting to feel unusual."

Ez'iri smiled. "That is not what I mean. Kinsman." She turned to Tai'en. "I leave you with your mate." Rayne's last lifeline ducked through the iris door all too quickly, and she was alone with Tai'en.

Chapter Nine

He walked slowly, making a tight circle around her
bound body. She chewed her lip and kept her head
down, all her energy focused on being a good girl. Out
of the corner of her eye, as he passed in front of her, she
stole glances at his bare, muscled legs. He really was a
treat to look at, even if his next move might be to kick
her butt from one end of the galaxy to the other.

"So I am to believe my mate awaits my pleasure
obediently?"

She nodded, keeping her eyes on the floor.

"Speak," he commanded.

"Yes," she said, hating the way her voice shook.

"Yes what?"

She remembered their time on his private craft,
when he forced her to ask for what she wanted. It hadn't
been easy, but the results had been worth it. "Yes, I
await my mate's pleasure." Her body lit up like a
Roman candle, the blush making itself felt all the way

down to her toes. The professional, clinical scientist in her packed its things and skipped town, leaving her lost and feeling more naked than she'd ever felt before, lack of physical clothing notwithstanding.

"My disobedient mate seeks my forgiveness?"

She nodded, then hastened to say, "I seek the forgiveness and understanding of my mate."

"My mate is willing to do whatever I command to earn that forgiveness?"

The quivery feeling in her stomach grew, and surprisingly, hints of anticipation danced with it, reaching out and liquefying her extremities. "I am," she began haltingly, "I am willing to do whatever…" oh, God, could she really say this? Could she mean it? "Whatever you command," she finished in a rush that sent fire burning from her neck to the roots of her hair.

He moved in front of her. Then he crouched down. His fingers, when they reached beneath her chin to tilt her head up, were gentle.

"You ran away from me," he said, pain in his voice. "You believed I would fail to hold what I have claimed."

"I had to keep a war from starting." Dammit! Wrong thing to say. She was supposed to be submissively earning his forgiveness. "I'm sorry," she said hastily.

"You didn't trust me," he said bluntly. "You didn't trust me to keep my men from abandoning our directive."

"I *did* trust you," she insisted, unable to keep her damn mouth shut. "I just didn't trust them. I'm sorry," she said again, "I'm making a mess of this submissive stuff."

"I have no doubt we will have plenty of opportunity for you to practice." His tone was wry. Hints of the Tai'en she first encountered relaxed her. She remembered that he had defied the wishes of his people for her, chose her after an extended period of celibacy, and not because of her intelligence, but because of something about her sexuality. After living her life on brain power alone, it meant something that he recognized more in her than just gray matter.

She lowered her head again. "I await your pleasure," she said. This time, she meant it.

The dynamic shifted and the air in the room grew heavy. "My mate seeks to please me with her obedience," he said. "But how shall she do that? Her hands are bound." He traced a finger along the laces holding her together.

She shivered. His touches were feather-light, but they awakened her sleeping beast. She arched her back when his finger danced over her spine.

He dropped his gaze to her jutting breasts and flicked his finger over her nipple. The sensitive nub hardened at his touch. "Your breasts please me," he said. "Offer them to me."

Limited in movement as she was, the best she could do was arch her back even further and lift her hips. She gasped as the laces slid along her inner flesh once again. Sudden and powerful need to have his mouth on her nipples seized her.

"Gifts are not presented without some indication as to what they are used for," he said.

She swallowed again. Dizzy with the effort it took to actually form the words, she stuttered, "I off-offer you m-my breasts."

"What would you have me do with them?"

Oh God. "Suck on them. Please." She was burning now, the blood in her veins replaced with hot lava that bubbled and flowed in a burning path between her breasts and her pussy.

He moved closer to her, heat radiating from his body. Her nipples strained to make contact. Her awkward arch kept her from initiating the contact. It was all up to him.

His body shifted and rippled with subtle color movements, purpling as his gaze flicked over her offered body.

The hot fullness between her legs grew until she could bear it no longer. She nudged her knees apart at the same time as his tongue flicked out to curl around her nipple. The laces slid against her flesh, pulling at her clit. Heat shot through her and she came, suddenly, startlingly, with a small cry, her pussy convulsing around nothing.

Hunger and need overwhelmed her, shaking her quivering limbs. He slid one finger inside her creamy wetness, stroking her throbbing clit with his thumb. "You come for me," he said.

Her body taut as a bowstring, she met his eyes. "I come for you."

Yet she needed more. She knew it, and he knew it, too. He pulled his finger out of her pussy and drew her creamy wetness over her anus. She flexed and trembled. "Oh, yes," she whispered.

He slid the tip of his finger inside her and she moaned. Then he withdrew it again. "Does my willing mate seek to please me," he asked, "or herself?"

The wrong answer to this question would be a disaster, she thought. "I seek to please you," she said. "Pleasing you pleases me."

"Tell me, then, what will bring us pleasure?"

Fuck me senseless, she thought. It was too much of a command. "I want," she started, then rephrased it. "No, wait." She spread her legs wider. "I offer my pussy to you. And my ass." The mere words had the power to make her quiver. "I am open and ready to take your cocks."

His yellow eyes were twin flames as the lilac flush spread over his body. He growled. She smiled invitingly. There was a certain power in submission, she realized, in the knowledge that she trusted him to please her. "Show me how open you are," he commanded.

She couldn't arch backwards any further, but she could bend forward. When she did, she discovered a sensual bonus to her bonds. The laces that ran down either side of her clit drew taut as her cheek touched the floor in front of her, and when she lifted up her bottom to give him her pussy, the laces held her labia open for him. The completely submissive posture alone made her come again, little shivers that rocketed from her throbbing pussy out into her fingers and toes and back.

He moved around behind her and even though she couldn't see, she felt his hot gaze on her private parts, open for display. She waited for his touch, for the feel of his cocks sliding into her, but only cool air and anticipation greeted her. "Tai'en?"

"I am admiring what belongs to me."

If he didn't take her right now, she'd explode. His gaze moved over her palpably and she shifted in desperation. She felt him lean over her. His bone spurs brushed against her back. "Will you accept punishment from me?"

Shivers raced through her. Up until now, the submission had been a game. Now she couldn't forget that in spite of the love play, he hadn't yet told her he'd forgiven her.

She wanted to protest. She didn't deserve punishment for trying to protect her planet.

"I cannot forgive your transgression until punishment is meted out," he said, as if he sensed her hesitation.

She whimpered. Her body begged for hard release, yet she wanted to argue her innocence. *But this isn't about guilt and innocence*, she realized. *This is about dominance and submission, and I'm the submissive one.*

Did she trust him enough to let him punish her? Slowly, she nodded her assent. She trusted him with her fate.

The sharp sting of his hand on her bottom sent a shock through her that felt like hot water hitting ice cubes. She let out an undignified yelp. His hand came down again. This time, she bit her lip and accepted her punishment like a good girl.

Several more smart spanks and he finally leaned down to whisper into her ear. "Will you run from me again?"

She gasped for breath. Her rear end was on fire and her first instinct was to scream, "Hell, yes, you bastard!" and not only run, but run screaming out the nearest airlock and let the cold of space soothe the burning on her butt.

But his hand turned caressing, and the sting faded, leaving a heated tingling where the pain used to be. The sudden dip of his finger into her pussy sent waves of incredible, intense liquid pleasure through her. "Will you run from me?" he repeated.

She shook her head. "No." Her humiliation didn't seem so important in the face of the pleasure radiating out from her core.

"Good," he said, and he gave her what she craved, filling her front and back and summoning the aching need within her to be tamed.

Unable to move with her bonds limiting her, she could do nothing more than accept the pleasure he gave her with each thrust. He made her twist and squirm. The laces binding her squeezed and chafed with delicious friction along her clit and labia. He made her beg, and when she finally came, it was by his command. "Come for me now, Insatiable One."

She screamed as orgasm rippled through her. He nipped the back of her neck with his teeth as he joined her in pleasure, grinding out a single word against her skin.

"Mine."

When she came down from the orgasm, not even her bonds could keep her limbs from shaking violently. He undid the laces and unwound them from her body with gentle hands. Blood returned to her fingers and toes with a painful rush and she groaned.

He gathered her into his arms and stretched out with her on the sleeping couch, covering her with a light throw. With her thundering desire temporarily quieted, the humiliation of her actions returned to her in full force. How could she behave so—so wantonly, how could she debase herself so? She turned away from him.

"Rayne'iri," he said gruffly.

"That was humiliating," she said bluntly. "You treated me like a child!"

"That was most definitely not child's play."

"It was still humiliating."

"Why must you attach guilt to pleasure?"

"Damned if I know."

"You are a proud woman, my mate." Humor evident in his voice, he turned her to face him. "Your trust is not easily won. It is a gift."

She searched his eyes. Like his skin, blue-tinged with affection, they held nothing disturbing that she could see.

Was it only pride that kept her ashamed of her sexual escapades?

"Why did you return to me?"

The sudden change of subject threw her. So did the thread of uncertainty in his voice. "I don't…" Actually, she did know. It would just take the abandoning of every shred of her pride to say it. "I…" God, she didn't even know if the Alcaini had a word for love in their language, or how their culture treated the notion. Ironically, Kenneth could now sit back and be right about her clinical detachment being limiting. "Tai'en, my people have this thing called love, and I love you. That means being with you."

"Do you think we know nothing of love?" His voice turned hard. His eyes were harder. "Do you think my people have driven ourselves to the brink of extinction for anything besides love?" His skin rippled with color, flushing from yellow, to orange, then to the lilac of arousal, all the way to a deep, mottled indigo-violet. "Do you believe simple biological urges motivate us and nothing else?"

She shook her head. "I—I don't know. I used to think they motivated everybody, human, Alcaini, or whatever. I know differently now."

"The love I have in me for you has no mate in you without your trust," he said.

"You have it," she said. The words he spoke—more eloquent than any she'd ever heard, even in the sappiest movies—reached inside her and pulled at her heart.

"You must prove it," he said. His eyes smoldered.

"How? What was that we just did then?"

"That was private," he said. "That was for me. But I am not the only Alcaini to think of. My people do not approve of my choice as a mate."

"So I hear." And now that she would be depending on the goodwill and wishes of Tai'en's people, she had a vested interest in changing their minds. "What do you have in mind?"

"Do you trust me? Truly?"

"Yes," she said, confident now in their shared fate.

"Then share our mating. In Communion."

She should have kept her mouth shut. Basking in the afterglow of incredible sex and emotional upheaval was not the time to be promising new and adventurous experiments in sex. She had little time to regret her agreement, though. Tai'en made the announcement to Ez'iri when she joined them for the next meal. As Rayne stirred a clear, orangey soup that tasted like chicken, which meant it could be virtually anything, Tai'en told Ez'iri they would be sharing their next mating in a Communion.

Ez'iri was so shocked she dropped her goblet of flower juice. She stuttered something in Alcaini, then ran from the room.

"She goes to prepare," Tai'en said, as if that explained everything. He smiled. "Once word of a Communion reaches the ears of my fellow Alcaini, it will be all we can do to beat them back. As my closest kin, Ez'iri will have the honor of hosting the event. As I have told no one but her, and maintained the utmost secrecy about our Communion, little time will pass before the entire ship knows about it."

He made it sound like a party. She couldn't help but smile at the image of Ez'iri drifting through a group of elegantly-attired Alcaini. "Canape? Oral sex?" A laugh, perhaps the tiniest bit hysterical, escaped her. She peered around at the others in the feast hall and remembered Irek'iri's comments about Communion.

How many Alcaini here had ever been to one before? What would they think of it—of her? She'd have to look each and every one of them in the eye afterwards—could she really go through with an orgy?

Ez'iri met with her at the end of the feast. "There is little for you to do in preparation, but I will take you to a private room to do so."

"You mean, we're going to have the Communion *now*?" she squeaked, panic once again taking up residence in the middle of her chest.

"How do you say it? The wheels already turn."

Her friend led her to small living quarters, obviously meant for someone with little rank. But even the most common Alcaini still merited a bathtub. Memories of her last bath aboard the Alcaini ship gave her pause.

Ez'iri met her eyes. A small smile danced around her lips. "This bath, you take alone," she said.

"This Communion—I know it involves public mating, but I get the feeling everyone's leaving something unsaid."

Ez'iri waited a long moment before speaking. She punched the panel in the wall that controlled the water that pooled into the bathing tub, and turned it three different colors before she finally spoke. "The elders of us…do not approve of Communion."

"That sounds a little prudish for your culture."

"It isn't the sex," she said. "Our urge to mate outside our species is strong. Since our population began dying out, those urges have grown stronger, and the shame attached to them has grown to match it. It is as if every new generation is doomed to experience hungers more immoral than the last. The elders try to shame us into mating with our own kind. But too many still know about Communion and its effects."

Rayne sank into the tub. "And what, exactly are those effects?"

"For you, they are little. For us, it is Communion." She shrugged. "We return to a time when the hearts and minds of our clans were as one."

Ez'iri's words were poetic, but not very forthcoming. "Meaning?"

"During a Communion, we think and feel as one." Ez'iri's voice grew dreamy. "We will all be with Tai'en as he claims his mate."

"Sounds like empathy of a sort."

"One could call it that. It is theorized that our people used to have this ability at all times, but much has been lost with the decline of our population." She glowed a lovely shade of turquoise excitement. "Rayne'iri, you are truly magnificent amongst females. Communion is an act beyond generosity. Twice now, you have gifted me with great honor." She placed her hand up, palm facing out.

Rayne put her own hand against her friend's, the contact warm, and remembered her first gift of the information about in-vitro fertilization. "Tell me—will the first gift help you at all?"

Ez'iri smiled. "It has given me some comfort." She lowered her voice. "I have shared it with another like-minded Physician. We plan to quietly begin our own study."

She couldn't keep the smile from her face. "I'm so happy to hear that." Perhaps some good would come out of Human-Alcaini relations after all.

She straightened, pragmatic once again. "I will leave you now to your bath."

* ~ *

Her bath water cooled far too quickly. Ez'iri returned to clothe her in a short, plain tunic. "Easier for running," she explained.

Rayne swallowed. She remembered what she'd told Kenneth back on Earth. *The Alcaini hunt their mates.* Maybe she hadn't been lying at all. Ez'iri pulled laces from her pouch and Rayne frowned. "Not more binding," she protested. She didn't know if her nerves could take another session like that.

Ez'iri smiled. "This is for your hair."

Rayne pulled the thick red mass over her shoulder and braided it quickly, tying off the end in a bushy pouf. Strands still hung in her face and on her neck, but most of it would be out of her way.

"Are you well-prepared for Communion?" Ez'iri asked when she flipped her braid over her shoulder.

How the hell should I know? "I think so." There was no going back, so she may as well go forward.

"Then let us go." Ez'iri led her out through the iris door into a long, discreetly lit corridor.

"Any last-minute instructions?" she asked, her nerves growing tighter by the second.

Ez'iri strode beside her with purposeful steps, but she remained silent for quite some time. "Trust your instincts," she said finally.

Not the answer she was looking for. Her instincts told her to run the other direction. Rayne looked at the walls. How big was this ship, anyway? For the past five minutes, they'd been walking down a curving corridor, dotted with iris doors, all of which they passed right by. "Okay, then. What am I supposed to do—besides the sex? Belis'iri and Irek'iri couldn't tell me anything." A sub-aural thumping began to make itself known to her through the soles of her bare feet. Maybe it was a problem with the ship's engines and the whole thing would be canceled due to technical difficulties.

"Communion is one of our oldest ceremonies. There are echoes of our people at the dawn of our race. We were not always a peaceful people." Ez'iri's voice had a faraway quality to it.

"Humans still aren't," she said. Her nerves were winding tighter with each step, and her friend wasn't helping.

"Communion predates our civilization," she said.

"But I thought you only did this thing with aliens?"

"My words were inaccurate, then. Communion…calls to the Alcaini spirit that lives outside of the laws of society. Does that explain?"

"Do you mean to say it brings out the primitive in you?"

Ez'iri took two more doors to consider that. "Yes. That seems to translate accurately. She stopped at the last iris door. "Communion was not always labeled as such."

The door began to iris open. "What was it call…" Her question trailed off as she beheld the other side of the curved wall. A room the size of a concert hall, with three tiers rising from the center out to the walls, held hundreds of Alcaini. A wall of sound hit her, the thump revealing itself to be not the engines of the ship, but hundreds of drums playing in rhythm that reached down her throat and grabbed her by the very cells in her body. "Oh my God!" She backed up.

A solid chest stopped her and she whirled. Tai'en had materialized behind her and her breath stopped. Besides a loincloth, his only other covering was an intricately criss-crossed series of leatherlike straps roping his arms, legs, and torso. But it was his skin that arrested her breathing. The faint rosettes she'd noticed before were more pronounced, deep burgundy striations against his crimson-red skin. The dark mottling seemed to pulse in time to the blood flowing in her own veins, calling it forth unconsciously.

"Lady," he said. His voice was harsh, deep. Gooseflesh rose on her skin at hearing it.

She could feel his heart adjusting its beat to the pulse of the drumming, and her own desire to follow along. But—*all these people!* "I can't do this!" She panicked. "There's too many people here."

"You must, 'iri." His voice was not the calm and sensual deepness she'd come to expect. "This cannot be undone."

"I thought this was a small gathering of hand-picked relatives! Who's left to run the ship?" Something palpable in the air fixed itself on her panic. The drumming picked up speed and she felt his muscles tense and coil. The urge to run suddenly overwhelmed her, along with a host of other urges—to chase, conquer, dominate, submit…mate. The Alcaini began a chant, a word she couldn't recognize. She clutched at his arms. "What's happening?" she shouted above the din of drums and chanting.

"It is the Communion," Ez'iri said. "As I said, before we called it the Communion, it went by another name."

Irek'iri appeared before them. "It is time," she shouted. "Rayne'iri, you must run as fast as you can. Use your wits and your senses. A too-easy conquer will be disastrous for a Communion as large as this one."

The onslaught of emotions and impulses literally made her muscles twitch with the effort of keeping herself focused on one thing. She turned to Tai'en. His eyes gleamed in the dim light. Her heart accelerated. "What?" she said, breathing deep with the effort of fighting the swept away feeling that threatened to drown her. "What was the Communion called before?"

Beside her, Ez'iri gasped. "Rayne'iri, you must run now!"

Tai'en dropped into a crouch. "It was called," he growled, "the hunt."

Chapter Ten

Rayne didn't think. She ran. The lights went out as she took off through the crowd. The chanting stopped, and cheering began. Everywhere she ran, the drums followed her, thrumming into her brain, seeping into her consciousness.

The hands and bodies around her flowed in a sub-rhythm in time with the drumming. All she could see were the many glowing eyes of the Alcaini, flashing in the darkness. What she felt, however, pumped her legs faster.

Sensations slammed into her from every direction. Her skin crawled with the need to touch, and touched she was—hands, bodies, petted her in fleeting touches and long strokes. Heavy sexual need pulsed in her body in counterpoint to her heartbeat. And behind her, somewhere, she could feel Tai'en. His hot breath seemed to always be brushing her neck, his powerful body just a step behind, a heartbeat away from taking her down.

The crowd parted. Instinctively, she jumped, and was rewarded by a hard landing on the first tier. She switched directions, a fresh frisson of fear spiking through her. She ran along the first tier's great arc, feeling the building frenzy of the Alcaini around her. Each of them projected their anticipation of her capture and submission, which fueled her own desire to keep running.

Lord only knew how long she could keep running like this. She couldn't see and her lungs felt like they were about to explode with the pulsebeat of the drums and the exertion of her body. Her fear, her terror that any moment, his hands would slam down on her shoulders and pin her to the ground, rolled off her in waves, and the people around her lapped it up like sweet syrup.

The connection was by no means one-way, however. As her feet pounded on the hard floor, she felt the web of connection binding her to the entire room. It wasn't her own senses that told her she was dangerously close to falling off the ledge, or that if she jumped *just now*, she could clear the first tier and hit the second.

Around her, she felt the ebb and flow of people, their excitement feeding her own. Any second now, he would pounce, and the chase would be over. She burst through the other side of fear, into that fatalistic anticipation that begged for the fear to be realized, so at least the wait would finally be over. Her dodges and bursts of speed began to energize her—her cleverness stimulated her and before long, she was laughing with a kind of reckless joy so intense that it sang in her skin and sinews and bones, swelling her consciousness beyond her body and out into the room, so it seemed perfectly natural for her in her flight to suddenly leap sideways into open airspace.

Cool air caressed her skin as she fell towards the floor. She knew landing would hurt. It didn't matter—pain, pleasure, sensation, they were all part of this consciousness experience. *I just hope I don't bounce.*

She didn't bounce. She didn't even hit the floor. Instead, she hit solid, heated chest bound by leather straps. Arms whipped around her, pinning her against him as they both fell. His cry of triumph echoed through the room, sounding over the drums.

She didn't hit the ground, but he did—hard, and the impact traveled through him to her. The shock of physical contact—of his actual capture and claim of her, called to her most primitive fight-or-flight instincts and she twisted in his arms, fighting like hell to free herself from his embrace. The light garment that covered her knotted and tore, exposing her flesh to the crowd.

Quick as lightspeed, he flipped and pinned her to the floor. Her arms were held out from her body. Hands grasped her wrists and restrained them against the floor. He slid down against her until his body lay nestled between her legs.

More hands reached for her ankles, sliding over her skin and pulling her legs apart until she was spread-eagled before him and the rest of the crowd.

The feeling of absolute helplessness burned her, and she strained against the hands that held her down. But the hands were unrelenting. She sought out the pair of glowing yellow eyes that belonged to her captor. The collective emotions of the crowd screamed through her nerve endings, some urging her to put up a fight, some demanding that now was the time to submit. She grew confused at the onslaught and closed her eyes, wishing her hands were free to press over her ears. It's too much, she thought frantically. The hands that held her wrists and ankles tightened against her struggles.

Panic rolled off her and returned to her magnified until she screamed, sure her skin would swell and burst with hysteria. Except for the hands holding her bound, only one large hand remained, the rest withdrew.

His hand lay heavy on her stomach, just above her mons, leaving a heated imprint of possession. Strangely, she was reassured by it. Whatever else happened to her in the crowd, it would happen to him in some way, too.

Something snapped, some tide turned, and her panic began to recede, leaving in its wake the rest of the sensations associated with being bound. Incredibly, the immobility became exciting. She had fought long and hard, run fast and dodged cleverly, yet the inevitable had finally come to her.

The chanting and cheering quieted, the drums subsided to a slow, pulsing heartbeat, and a watchful tension entered the air, tightening her body with anticipation. The warmth of his hand spread from her lower abdomen outward, centering between her legs and heating the pulse in her throat until she was breathless. The movement she sensed more than saw slowed until the entire room shared her expectancy.

She waited for what seemed like a lifetime before he moved again. His other hand joined his first, possessive one on her belly. They spread out and stroked around her hips, moving down her hips and around the outside of her thighs. The press of bodies was so rife with presence that it merged into a single cocoon around her.

His hands stroked her legs, at first slowly, then with increasing speed. She somehow knew he was memorizing the feel of her, from the roundness of her thighs to the bones that jutted out from her ankles, the scar on her kneecap, the springy pubic hair that teased his fingers. She didn't know how long he stroked her body, running his fingers up the sides of her ribs, tickling her, down her arms, over her breasts, pausing to tweak her nipples to stiff attention. He paid particular attention to her mons, stroking in between her pussy lips until they swelled and parted, exposing her sensitive clitoris. *Oh, yes*, she thought. *Touch me there, please!*

He obliged, but it wasn't nearly enough. He circled the bud with his fingers, flicking it this way and that, then dipped one finger into her slit with a sudden thrust that took her by surprise. She lifted her hips invitingly.

Her efforts were futile, however, and he withdrew his finger. She made a small sound of disappointment that turned into a startled gasp as that same finger thrust into her ass. She moaned as a small ripple of pleasure rolled over her. But he denied her even that, pulling his finger away.

He then commenced to start the process all over again, starting with her hips, this time using his fingernails, tracing light scratches all over her body. By the time he reached her clit the second time, her entire body was on fire and she ached to be completed, filled, touched, mounted, *anything* to uncoil the tension wound tight within her.

He stopped with a light scratch around her outer labial folds. And then he left her.

She ground her teeth together, a long, frustrated groan coming out of the back of her throat. The absence of his presence left coldness around her, and she grew very aware of her exposed, *vulnerable* position.

She saw through the eyes of the Alcaini—eyes that could see clearly in the dark, and saw herself spread-eagled, body glistening with sweat, nipples jutting proudly, pussy lips pink and wide open. This had to be worse than what Kenneth had done to her—at least she could hide from the speculation generated by his theories about her sexuality. But this—her sexuality was on display, and there was nowhere she could hide.

Even with her eyes shut, she could still see herself. In fact, closing her eyes brought the image of herself into sharp focus. She could even feel the curiosity they felt about her *iriwai*—her vagina—and its single, tight opening, their speculation about her anus, their fascination with her difference from them.

She was a freak. She couldn't find happiness with anyone in her entire species! She wanted to sink into the floor, away from the hard truth that she sought out unholy fulfillment with strange beings. Shame burned deep in her belly, spreading out and raging alongside the desire to couple and all the other emotions swamping her senses.

She tried to curl in on herself, but hands materialized around her, stroking her skin, petting her hair, and a sense of wonderment overrode the shame. These people celebrated her difference, she realized. They held it in respect and admired it. They were collectively, genuinely puzzled as to why she didn't do the same.

Her willingness to look beyond her own kind had led her to become part of something beyond human experience. The other side of her stark raving terror of herself was—arousal. Her arousal reached out and received an answer from the crowd, magnifying and intensifying until her very flesh sang with reckless abandon.

The sudden feel of his lips on her nipple shocked her. She arched into his mouth, the adrenaline from the chase, the sensory awareness brought on by the combination of deprivation and over-stimulation focused itself in an arrow-sharp hunger for release. She no longer cared about where they were, who was watching, or what kind of wrong it was to delight in her own behavior.

The hands that had returned to comfort her now turned to arousal. Fingers plucked at her nipples, stroked her inner thighs, slid between her pussy lips. She felt the touch of a tongue on her clit and knew it wasn't Tai'en. Tongues tasted her flesh, dipping in and out of her pussy, firing her nerve endings in rapid-fire explosions. Hands stroked, scratched, pinched her nipples, sending bolts of sensation back and forth between herself and the others clustered around her.

The drums once again increased in their intensity. Over the thrumming, she heard his voice in her head. "I claim this body as mine, to mate and mount. No desires but mine, and no pleasures but mine." Even in her head, and in the intense environment, she heard the desperate edge to his voice.

"Yes," she replied, heart welling up into her throat. Through the raging possessive tide of his desire, she felt a thread of tenderness for her.

The helping hands loosened around her ankles and bent her knees for her. Her pussy was open and exposed, her hips lifted and she opened herself to take him. Hands and arms supported her, lifting her torso and sliding under her hips. Fingers probed and spread her cheeks, occasionally dipping into her pussy or ass for an exploratory thrust. Knowing the thrusts were illicit only made them more exciting.

Her passage dripped, creamy wet and quivering, desperate to be filled. She was lifted, supported by many hands and arms in a web of humanity—not humanity, she corrected herself, Alcaini-ness. Being-ness. Her head dropped back, overwhelmed by the sensuality of it all. "Take me," she begged.

A low growl in her head was her answer. The initial twin thrusts of his cocks entering her holes took her breath away on a long scream of ecstasy.

She'd never been taken by him this way before. Her back was arched back while her hips tilted forward to accommodate him. Her body felt stretched, her muscles shaking with the exertion of holding herself for his pleasure. The many arms that supported her helped, but didn't allow her much purchase. He thrust into her and her support network held firm.

His thrusts stoked her higher. Her pussy swelled plump, tightening around him. Her rear muscles stiffened and relaxed in time with his thrusts. Her clit throbbed, the friction of his cock teasing it to a maddening ache. Through it all, the sensations she flung out echoed back to her, the desires of the Alcaini around her magnifying her own.

An orgasm hit her suddenly, tightening every muscle and ending in a sharp scream from her throat. *Nooo…* she thought, *it's too soon!*

Her disappointment was short lived, though. No sooner did her orgasm subside then another one crashed over her, flooding her cunt with juices and stretching her ass open for him to go deeper. His hips pistoned into her and greedy desires took over her thoughts and feelings. All she wanted was more—more of him, more of the sensations rocking her body, more hands and arms and bodies supporting her, more touches. "Give me more," she begged, "I want it all!"

His hips pistoned against her. It still wasn't enough. With a mighty burst of strength, she pulled one of her hands free and clapped it around his neck. She pulled him down on top of her. Beneath her, the hands and arms and bodies strained to support the additional weight.

Her mouth found his. The shock of contact rippled through her as her tongue twined with his. She felt what he felt—the little electric sparks where her tongue touched his. She'd had no idea how sensitive the forks of his tongue were. It excited her. She closed her lips around it and sucked at it.

The shudder that ripped through him echoed in the crowd. Her hands searched for and found the spurs on his lower abdomen. Howls echoed through the crowd, and she felt little sparks and surges as the Alcaini on the outer edges of the crowd gave into the urge to mate.

Tai'en threw his head back and roared, the sound sweeping through her both inside and outside of her head. He tore his lips from hers and buried his face in her neck and bit down hard.

In that instant, she lived for him, breathed and existed for this moment, and the answering spurt of satisfaction when her own teeth dug into his flesh.

The taste of him filled her mouth. He roared, thrusting hard as his seed spurted into her. Her body answered his, arching as the hardest orgasm of her life hit her with waves of pleasure so intense they were painful. The waves flooded out of her into the crowd and came back. Screams and howls echoed through the room, in time with the drums and her careening pulse.

The come crested and her skin split apart, a long scream ripping from her throat as her body finally exploded into a million stars. Each star exploded into a million more until her consciousness expanded to the room then to the ship, then outside to the universe itself, all of it contained in each convulsion of her body until there was nothing left but the drumbeat in the darkness, and glowing Alcaini eyes.

* ~ *

She came back to herself some time later in a much smaller room, alone in blessed silence. She felt like she'd been put through a wringer, and almost wished her bizarre immune system hadn't fought off the toxic microbes Kenneth injected into her. Death would be sweet surcease from the aching in her limbs. She was sore everywhere—her joints, her muscles, her breasts, her pussy. Hell, her legs still wouldn't close properly. But rather than annoyance, she could only summon up a fond smile at the thought. She'd been a part of something special, and she couldn't feel regret over it. Perhaps shame would come later, but she'd deal with that when she had more than a scant handful of brain cells.

She was on a couch, she finally noted, after staring at the muted light emanating from the wall sconces for what seemed like an hour. The couch wasn't a medi-couch, but similar in its decadent lounging function. When she pulled her eyes away from the hypnotic light, she saw there was a low table in front of her. A bowl of scented water and cloths lay on the table, next to a decanter of flower juice for her interminable thirst. *Oh, thank heavens*, she thought. Her mouth tasted like, well, she didn't want to speculate on what it tasted like, she thought, remembering the animalistic way she'd bitten into his flesh while she came.

As she sat up, a hollow ache roared to life, burning in her belly and sending waves of dizziness to blacken the edges of her field of vision. She reached for the decanter and missed, crashing to the floor, flower juice spilling everywhere.

The iris door opened and Tai'en walked in. "Rayne'iri!"

"I'm okay," she mumbled groggily. Purple flower juice stained her skin, leaving sticky residue everywhere. Not that she was sparkling clean beforehand, but the flower juice wasn't helping.

He moved the table, splashing water from the basin, and knelt beside her. "You should have called for an attendant. Belis'iri or Irek'iri would have come to you immediately."

She remembered the rolling orgasm that came from her first bath aboard the vessel. "Like they did last time?" She grimaced. "There's a point where it all becomes too much. I reached that point about twelve hours ago. I think. How long was I out?"

He dipped a cloth into the steaming, scented water and wrung it out. "About an hour. Ordinarily feasting would not commence until the guests of honor returned to the room, but you showed no signs of consciousness before now. Ez'iri thought it prudent to begin the feasting without us." He began to bathe her body in long, smooth strokes.

She melted under his touch. "Apart from the amazing telepathic group sex, it sounds a lot like a human wedding celebration," she said dryly.

He rubbed the cloth over her legs, stroking up between her thighs. *God, I don't know when to quit, do I?* She thought as wetness not from the washcloth drenched her pussy. She looked into his eyes and found an answering glow of desire there.

"We cannot possibly," he said in a regret-tinged voice.

She smiled. "We could. I'd pay for it later, but we could."

He ran the cloth over her belly. It responded with a growl worthy of an Alcaini warrior, and he laughed. "This is one hunger that my cocks will not feed, my insatiable one. Come, and we will feast with those who have shared with us."

She held out one tired hand. "Before we go out there, you owe me a few answers."

He grasped her hand in his and pulled her up. Her legs didn't seem to want to cooperate and she slumped back into his arms the minute he tried to let go. They ended up half reclining on the couch, his arms wrapped around her as she rested her body against his. It was, she realized, a while since she'd been really held by anybody.

"What are the questions I must answer?" His voice rumbled in his chest. The beat of his heart was solid and reassuring against her cheek.

"During the Communion, I felt feelings I never felt before—feelings outside the range of human emotions.

I saw myself through at least a dozen different pairs of eyes." She twisted around to look him in the eye. "I thought Alcaini didn't display significant instances of telepathy." At the beginning of the research exchange with the alien race, there hadn't been a person among the research team who hadn't been at least a little relieved that the Alcaini couldn't read minds.

"It is a kind of empathy we experience, during the Communion. We believe it stems from the primitive time when our people hunted mates the same way we hunted prey. Alcaini women are not inclined towards monogamy. Males assured the fidelity of their mates through a combination of mental willpower and sexual enticement. At some time, the two combined and Communion became a way to ensure physical fidelity while allowing mental poly-fidelity for our females."

It became a little clearer why he was so fascinated with human women. "But I thought Communions only happen when Alcaini mate with outworlders."

"That is true. But my people mate with each other all the time. The desires we feel to mate with those not of our race are—different. More intense."

She didn't know how she felt about hearing that. This elaborate trap of trouble she was in all seemed to stem from the urge to mate outside her own kind. To know that what could have been a simple fantasy sim instead took a left turn at the corner of Bizarre and Deviant because of a biological urge—her woman's heart, unused as it was, protested.

The biologist in her was fascinated. *All of life stems from biological urges*, she said to herself. *They're simply magnified, socialized, and institutionalized into acceptable and not acceptable behavior, desirable circumstances, and societal norms.*

Her belly rumbled again, interrupting the philosophical side-trip her mind had taken. "You mentioned a feast," she said, struggling to get up.

He rose, bringing her with him. On a hook by the door, her kimono hung, and he plucked it from its peg and draped it around her shoulders. Why hadn't she noticed she was naked?

The iris door opened onto the giant room where the sharing had taken place, only the room had been transformed from a nightmarish jungle with a drumbeat to a large banquet hall. Drums still lined the top tier of the room, with occasional Alcaini rising from their cushions at low banquet tables to play a few rhythms or a short solo.

Good God, there were a lot of people there! She leaned into Tai'en. "Were all these people at the Communion?"

He nodded. Her face burst into fire. Every single one of these people had seen her naked, felt her desires—unholy as they were—witnessed her brains getting fucked out of her ears, and reveled in it. She wanted to sink through the floor.

She turned around and dove for the iris door.

Ez'iri and Tai'en both caught her by an arm. "Rayne'iri, my friend, what troubles you?"

"Troubles me? Troubles me!" Her voice rose to a shrill pitch of hysteria. "I'm going to die of shame, that's what troubles me. You wasted your time curing me of those microbes—I'm going to melt and my brains are gonna leak out my ears!"

Ez'iri's hand automatically went to the shell of her ear. "Your aural canals do not appear inflamed."

"Oh, for Pete's sake!" Now was not the time for Ez'iri to go obtuse on her. "I can't face these people, knowing what I did—how I acted—in front of them. It's all I can do to face you and Tai'en, and I know you!"

During her diatribe, a ripple had cut through the din of the room, and she became aware of eyes on her. Lots of eyes. A knot of young adult Alcaini passed by them. Several of them reached out a hand to touch her or Tai'en. The soft brushes of fingertips were accompanied by murmurs of "ozpeti." *Thanks.*

One young woman caught her eye. Her gaze glowed golden and it was plain to see, even through an interstellar cultural barrier, the joy and awe that radiated from her, which faltered at Rayne's own aggravated body language.

Rayne clamped her jaw closed. Whatever issues she had about her behavior earlier, she realized, belonged to her alone. She offered the girl a small smile.

"Ozpeti, 'iri," the girl said, reaching out fingertips to brush against her skin.

She nodded. The girl drifted off, whispering eagerly to her friends, their short kimonos fluttering in their excitement.

She took a deep breath and looked at Ez'iri and Tai'en. "Never mind," she said. "I'm ready to join the feast." She could damn well get over her hang-ups without taking it out on these people when they only wanted to celebrate.

For the rest of the feast, as she and Tai'en occupied places of honor at a table slightly apart from the rest, she smiled and talked—or tried to communicate—using her best behavior. Hands were constantly brushing over her hair or her skin, small touches by passers-by, or light strokes by some who'd approached her to do just that. She put up with it, and even welcomed it, a little, once she got used to it.

And she ate. Her body had been stretched to its limits in the past forty-eight hours, and she desperately needed fuel. Belis'iri assured her that everything at the feast had been hand-picked to conform to human dietary needs, or at least, she said with a sly smile, prove not to be incompatible. Rayne took advantage of the party atmosphere to stuff herself, the rumbling in her belly having turned to burning need.

All in all, it turned out to be the most bizarre wedding reception she'd ever been to. As the evening wound down, people began drifting out in pairs or small groups. She learned from Tai'en that they were expected to remain until the last guest had departed. "I feel like I should be passing out party favors," she muttered. Her eyelids began to droop.

Finally, long after the cows—or the Alcaini equivalent—had come home, they bowed to the last guest and Tai'en led her back to his quarters. He wrapped his powerful arms around her and they slept.

Chapter Eleven

It felt like only five minutes had passed before she roused at the sudden absence of warmth at her back.

Tai'en was pulling his armor from the trunk at the foot of the couch. "I must go."

"But it's only been five minutes," she protested.

"It's been hours, Lazy One." He smiled. "And this ship does not run itself."

Warmth flushed from her head to her toes at his smile. "What should I do?"

"Go back to sleep. When you have rested fully, Ez'iri will have something for you to do, I'm sure." He bent and kissed her, and for all the world she felt like a very bizarre June Cleaver waving Ward off to work. When she drifted back to sleep after he left, she dreamed about Alcaini in suits driving Chevys.

When she woke up for real, she contacted Ez'iri through the communicator panel. Ez'iri invited her to the biology lab to join in some research. As Rayne slipped on an Alcaini garment, she hummed. At least she had something of a job around here. She'd be unemployed back on Earth.

She left their quarters and started down a long hallway she thought was the right direction. Several turns later, she was hopelessly lost. No one passed her all this time, and she concluded she must be in some part of the ship used for storage. She came upon a door and palmed it open, to discover her instincts were correct. Boxes and containers line the walls of the small room, stacked two and three deep on top of one another. This room didn't even have one of the magic panels.

The next room she tried housed sleeping couches, low tables, and other assorted equipment that had been partially cannibalized. A furniture graveyard and someone's junk collection. She stepped further into the room, curious about the inner workings of a half-built medi-couch, she heard a noise in the hallway.

She was backing out of the room when a body slammed into her, sending her toppling to the floor with an, "Oof!"

The other body scrambled, kicking her in several places on its way off of her. She struggled to her feet and shock froze her limbs. "Kenneth!"

Her ex-boyfriend and perpetually-composed coworker was nearly unrecognizable. His hair was wild—even wilder than it was back when he'd been trying to cut her open. His face was streaked with something burnt-looking and his clothes were torn.

But the zap staff he held in his hand looked perfectly functional.

"Rayne," he said. "Just perfect. Go!" He prodded her with the zap staff.

"You don't even know how to use that thing," she said, annoyance with his antics more prevalent than fear.

His thumb stroked the base of the staff and it flared to life with a soft blue glow. "I'm a quick study, love. Now move. The alarms will sound shortly, and you'll make a fine hostage."

Well, hell. To make his point further, he prodded her. The stick sent a jolt of electricity through her body and convulsed her muscles. "Ow!" she cried, falling to her knees with pained shock. She glared up at him. "All right, all right. I'm moving."

He kept behind her down the long hallway. "Where are we going," she asked.

"I'm getting the hell off this ship," he said. "And you're coming with me to keep your friends from getting ideas."

"Kenneth, you're crazy. We're light-years away from Earth. Where will we go?"

He palmed open a large door. True to his words, the alarm klaxon began to sound. "The guard woke up," he muttered. He took her arm and pulled her through the door.

It miffed her that he knew his way around the ship better than she did, as he'd taken her straight to a docking bay.

The thought of being trapped in a small craft in the cold interstellar reaches of space made her uncomfortable. The thought of being trapped in that craft with Kenneth made her downright scared.

Kenneth palmed open the door of the shuttle closest to the huge door on the other side of the room. *That one leads to outer space*, she thought dizzyingly.

It was a really lousy time to realize the frailty and smallness of human life versus the universe. *Don't panic*, she told herself.

Too late, her self replied back as he pushed her into the craft. "You don't know how to fly this thing," she said, hysterical visions of exploding right there in the docking bay sending shakes through her limbs.

Kenneth didn't seem to have the same imagination. He sat in the pilot's seat and began pressing buttons at random. One of the buttons lit up the console panel, and sure enough, luck was with him—the fickle bitch—and the shuttle lurched to life. It hovered, the door hanging open, while the bay doors remained shut.

"Well, now what?" she said. He shocked her with the zap staff.

She shrieked, falling to the floor of the craft. Pain crested over her in waves, followed by a paralyzing numbness that took minutes to fade. Somewhere along the line, he must have thumbed the setting up higher.

Kenneth punched a few more buttons. Through the open shuttle door, she saw the door to the bay open and a troop of soldiers rush in. The shuttle began to move forward, towards the closed doors.

One of the soldiers shouted something and broke from the troop. With a running leap, he caught the open door of the shuttle and hoisted himself inside.

"Tai'en," she gasped from the floor.

He glanced down at her, worry evident in his eyes. The door closed behind him.

"It's opening," Kenneth said excitedly.

She felt something hot at the back of her head. The smell of burning hair filled the cabin. "Back off, alien," Kenneth said. His voice had gone cold. "I've got this thing on the highest setting. Keep coming at me, and I vaporize your whore's head."

Tai'en's eyes filled with fury, his skin going deep burgundy until he nearly blended in with the darkness. "You will die for this, human."

The shuttle shot through the open bay door with a sickening lurch. On its way out, it struck one of the sides and Tai'en fell backwards. Kenneth leaped out of the pilot's chair and pushed the end of the zap staff into Tai'en's midsection.

"No!" she screamed. A flare of blue light burned itself on her retinas. Tai'en's body arched backwards and he went still.

"You bastard! I'll kill you myself." She launched herself at Kenneth. He caught her and pinned her arms to her sides. Pain shot through her, but it was nothing compared to the pain that ripped through her heart. Tears burned her eyes and clogged her throat, mingled with the smell of burning ozone.

Kenneth staggered back into the pilot's seat, pulling her with him. As she jabbed an elbow into his side, she fell into the console. She sniffed as her eye caught Tai'en's crumpled form in the shadows. The ship's movements must have been jerky enough to jostle his body to a facedown position. It was an ignominious position for such a noble man.

Kenneth pointed the zap stick at her, dragging her attention away from her lover's body. "How, Rayne?" he asked.

"How what, you bastard?"

"How could you fuck one of them?"

"One of them?" Fury turned her voice icy cold. "I didn't just fuck one of them," she said, savoring the shocked look on his face. "I let dozens of them touch me, take me, in ways you couldn't even comprehend."

"That's disgusting."

"You're disgusting, with your irrational fear and your gullibility," she said viciously. "You never even considered that I was unhappy with you because of you, did you? And you never bothered to consider my feelings before you invented some psycho-babble to explain away the fact that you *suck* as a lover." Grief overrode any self-preservation instinct she might have had.

His face grew mottled red. "You bitch," he said. "I tried everything to please you. Nothing I did brought you closer to me."

"Maybe I knew back then how you'd betray me."

His face twisted with fury. "You betrayed the human race." He brought the stick down on her head.

Dammit, not again, she thought as her vision blurred and went black.

She awoke sometime later only to have Kenneth aim the zap staff at her and fire it off again. Blinding pain shot through her, followed by blessed unconsciousness. The process repeated itself twice more.

The next time she came to, she kept her head down and turned away from him. The sound of Kenneth's voice echoed in her ears and a bright glare coming from the viewscreen in the cockpit. She cautiously lifted her head a fraction, waiting for the zap staff again.

Dominating the black-fielded viewscreen was a familiar sight she never expected to see again. Planet Earth—specifically Asia and Africa—filled the screen. Kenneth's voice kept going on. He was talking on—a cell phone. How disappointingly mundane. "Yes, I've got one of their craft, Dr. Warren, and a dead alien. I'm bringing them all in for study…yes, Dr. Warren's alive…No…*No*…She's had intimate relations with the aliens. The psychological data is more valuable. Yes, I see…the craft appears to have an auto-pilot function preprogrammed to the Earth's coordinates…yes, it was fortuitous. No, I didn't think of that, sir. Yessir, it is our duty to prevent and defeat a full-scale invasion any way possible."

Pain stabbed her heart. She slid her gaze backwards to find Tai'en's form in the shadows. As her eyes searched, her broken heart dropped. He was gone.

Kenneth must have done something with his body. They'd said good-bye this morning so casually. She longed to have his arms around her one more time. If only—

No more room for if onlys, she thought grimly, as the shuttle hit the earth's atmosphere. The western half of Africa disappeared, the island of Japan whirled by, then the blue expanse of the Pacific grew until it filled the viewscreen.

The shuttle heated up. Her body was thrown against the base of the co-pilot's seat. The floor was hot and the ship began to shudder and shake. Her teeth rattled in her head.

Kenneth gripped the zap staff in one hand and the edge of the console in the other. His hand slipped and he tumbled out of the seat onto the floor next to her.

She struggled against the g-force of their approach, dragging herself to a sitting position. Blue water filled the viewscreen, getting clearer at an alarming rate of speed. She heard a thundering boom as something outside the shuttle broke away from it.

The blue began to gyrate wildly. Her head was going to split apart from the pressure. Pressure that built in her sinuses and made even her eyeballs ache. They were going to crash, and it was going to hurt like hell— provided they didn't get pureed on the way down.

Beside her, Kenneth pulled himself up again. He grabbed the control stick and held on for dear life. The shuttle still shook like crazy, but they stopped the nauseating spiral of their descent.

Just then, a whirl of red and black shot past her into Kenneth. She shrieked in terror until she realized it was an Alcaini. Her Alcaini.

He was alive! Joy filled her, in spite of the reality of their very short and percussive immediate future. She could die happy because he was alive.

Kenneth and Tai'en struggled, discharges of the zap staff lighting them with garish blue flashes. A tangle of limbs and bodies, thrown around by gravity's fickleness. She climbed into the pilot's seat and grabbed the control stick. "Tai'en, how do I stop this thing?"

"Yellow—yellow—urgh—green," he grunted.

She looked around the control pad. I hope he wasn't stuttering, she thought grimly as she punched the yellow sigil twice and the green glyph once.

The shuttle's trajectory evened out, but the shuddering didn't stop. "We're still going to crash," she shouted frantically.

Behind her, she heard a hard, sickening thud and the struggle ceased. She squeezed her eyes shut and prayed.

Tai'en's exhausted voice sent a rush of relief through her. "It is done."

She flung herself out of the pilot's seat and into his arms. "Oh, God, I wanted to die when Kenneth took you down!"

His arms closed around her. "The staff must have had a weak power cell."

She remembered her own pain at its hands. "Not weak enough. Let's get out of here."

He slid into the pilot's seat. "The craft is too badly damaged. We have to land it or we'll break apart with the effort of breaking out of Earth's atmosphere." His hands flew over the controls.

"We might have a reception waiting for us when we hit ground. I heard Kenneth talking to his partners."

"We are not without our own allies," he said. Pryt'en's face appeared suddenly, floating in a disembodied hologram to the right of the viewscreen. He spoke in Alcaini to Tai'en. Tai'en replied, then turned to Rayne. "Harness yourself," he said, snapping himself in.

She pulled the harness of the co-pilot's seat over her head and around her waist, snapping herself in. It felt loose and she hoped the give was normal.

Seconds later, the heat became almost unbearable. "We may lose consciousness," Tai'en warned.

"I'm getting rather used to that," she retorted grumpily. With all the bumps on her head, she was surprised she didn't have brain damage already.

The shudders of the shuttle increased, along with the pressure that sent blood pounding into her head and behind her eyes. She could no longer keep a long groan from escaping her lips as her lungs fought against the pressure. Gray spots flooded her vision. *I will not pass out*, she thought, fighting the urge to close her eyes.

Her head jerked back and forth along with her body, and she gripped the sides of the chair, her muscles trembling with exertion. Just when she thought her teeth would rattle right out of her skull, the shuttle hit something that felt like a brick wall and the shuddering stopped.

After the whine of the engines and the sound of the shuttle shaking apart, the silence was deafening. She heard the lapping of water against the shuttle's hull. The control console smoked gently, sending ozone through the air like incense. "Tai'en?"

"I am unhurt. You?"

"I haven't fallen to pieces. Close, but not quite."

They lay there for a long minute, silently staring at the blue water and gray sky that filled the viewscreen. "Was it good for you, too?" she asked.

His laugh was strained. "You puzzle me, 'iri. You laugh when death is near and worry about minute details when it is not."

"It's all a matter of perspective."

"You fascinate me. I love you."

Her heart skipped. "Oh," she said, all melted inside. "If I didn't hurt so bad, I'd climb all over you and show you how much I love you."

"Pryt'en and the rest of the squadron will be here shortly to rescue us. It is certain that this is the last time we will be on your home planet. Are you sure you do not want to stay?"

"Take me home, Tai'en. Home is with the man I love." She waved the smoke away from her face and unsnapped her safety belt. The nose of the shuttle pointed upwards, sending everything not nailed down rolling to the back of the craft.

The hatch popped open with a hiss. She looked up, expecting to see a crimson and burgundy Alcaini face.

The face was blackened, all right, but it was war paint. "Dr. Taggart? Dr. Warren?"

Her eyes met those of a human man. She froze.

He slid inside the vessel, speaking into a throat microphone. "Target acquired. Securing perimeter of vessel. Confirm one survivor, seeking the—Holy Shit!" The man's eyes widened at the sight of Tai'en rising from the smoke.

He drew a wicked looking bowie knife from inside his black wetsuit. "Step away from the woman," he said in a firm tone.

Tai'en picked up Kenneth's abandoned staff and twirled it into a ready position. He wore a deadly look on his face. In the distance, she could hear the whut-whut of helicopter blades. "Ma'am," the man said stoically, "We're here to rescue you."

She offered him a smile. "Sorry, but I've already been rescued." Behind him, Pryt'en's head rose into view.

Pryt'en zapped him gently and he crumpled. Audible static emitted from his earpiece.

"Tai'en," she said. "He's got friends coming."

"Let us not linger," Tai'en said.

She stepped over the body of the military man and held her hands up to Pryt'en. As he lifted her out, she looked back towards the rear of the shuttle. Kenneth's body lay in a heap amid wall panels that had come loose and other detritus. She felt nothing for him. She might miss the planet, but she knew she had a lot more exciting adventures in her future, with a wonderful mate who loved her by her side.

"The shuttle is too badly damaged to recover. We will have to destroy it," Pryt'en said, once they were on board the second shuttle.

"Wait," she said.

His hand hovered over a blue glyph.

"Someone's inside that shuttle that doesn't deserve to die," she explained, thinking of the misguided guy who'd thought he was rescuing her.

Pryt'en said something in Alcaini. Tai'en replied, and they argued back and forth for a minute. Finally, Pryt'en shrugged and moved his hand away from the firing glyph.

Two Apache helicopters appeared on the shuttle's viewscreen. "Time to go," she said, pointing at them. One of the 'copters fired a halfhearted volley at them with little effect.

Pryt'en's hands flew over the controls and the shuttle executed a smooth turn and ascent, barely even registering on her sense of balance.

Rayne activated a smaller viewscreen at the back of the shuttle and kept her eyes fastened on the planet Earth until it shrank to a blue-green dot on an inky black field. As she reached to flip off the screen in a final goodbye, she felt Tai'en's arms around her. "We will travel several hours before arriving at the mother ship."

She turned in his arms and kissed him. His hands slid over her shoulders and down to cup her breasts. Liquid-cool desire filled her as his thumbs grazed her nipples. "Tai'en," she murmured, pulling away and glancing back towards the piloting cabin.

An answering tingle of awareness wiggled into her mind, not from Tai'en, but from the cabin, where she somehow, suddenly *knew* Pryt'en knew what they were doing back here.

"Do you know," Tai'en murmured, "that since our Communion, my clan has become rejuvenated?"

"Really?" What did that have to do with anything?

His hands stroked her thighs, sliding the hem of her short tunic up to expose her to his touch. His fingers danced along her flanks, dipping between her cheeks and around to tickle the sensitive skin of her lower abdomen. "Yes," he said, his voice as husky as his touch was light. "The elders are not happy that we held a Communion against their wishes. But the rest of us have new life in our veins. The younger members wish to continue our exploration of this sector, rather than returning to the homeworld."

She shivered as his finger stroked her clit. With his other hand, he stripped off her garment. And she gasped as she felt an answering, curious desire from Pryt'en.

Tai'en seemed not to notice anything amiss. "And there is talk of reviving more of the old ways. Our people were not always so focused on breeding."

Pryt'en's voice startled her. "In the old days," he said thickly, "Outworld mates were not a point of shame."

Crimson fire burned up her skin and she tried to pull away from Tai'en. "Pryt'en," she said, feeling more naked now than she had when he'd been assigned to drag her back to the scout ship after Kenneth had tried to dissect her. "Uhh…"

Tai'en's hands went to her shoulders. He slid his hands down her arms to her wrists and with a quick, deft movement, spun her around so that she faced Pryt'en, arms crossed in front of her and held in place by Tai'en's hands. His bone spurs pressed into the points on her bare back. Her breasts jutted forward, held up by her crossed arms.

Pryt'en reached out and captured a handful of her hair, rubbing the locks between his fingers. His skin shaded to violet as he leaned in close. His tongue flicked out, licking along her jaw, down her neck, into the hollow of her throat where her pulse accelerated.

Tai'en's cocks grew stiff, pressing against the cleft of her buttocks. She didn't need to look at him to know his body flushed with lavender desire. Pryt'en's tongue did not stop at her throat, though, and he continued the sensate flicking down to her breasts, over her peaked nipples. She held perfectly still, sure that the two men were in complete agreement, but unsure of her own place in the scheme of things. The empathy projected by the Alcaini didn't extend to exact thoughts, just emotions. "Tai'en?" she said, her voice shaking.

"It was not uncommon in past times," Tai'en murmured softly into her ear as Pryt'en continued his exploration down to the curly thatch of hair between her legs, "for us to seek pleasure for its own sake, in the many and varied ways open to us, especially with outworlders."

Pryt'en's forked tongue plunged into her curls, arrowing in on her clit. Her hips bucked involuntarily and a little moan escaped her lips. She could feel Tai'en's desire burning feverishly, and Pryt'en's fascination with her alien body.

Yet lingering doubt remained. In spite of the Communion, Tai'en was the only male she'd ever been with, and given the Alcaini—er, enhancements, there just wasn't room for everything.

Into her ear, Tai'en's hot breath carried his whispered words. "Do you trust me?"

Her doubt disappeared. "Yes."

He released her hands to slide his own down to her thighs. He opened her legs and Pryt'en delved his tongue into her pussy, sending shivers through her. She let out a long, drawn-out moan as the forks of his tongue whirled and tickled deep inside her.

Tai'en's finger dipped into her pussy, drawing her juices to the tight bud of her ass. Desire roared to full waking life within her and she lost the last bit of hesitation about Pryt'en's presence.

He was fascinated with her, and she returned the favor. His bone spurs held a slightly different pattern than Tai'en's, and she leaned over to explore them with her lips and tongue. Pryt'en was not as thickly muscled as her mate, but his body had a spare ranginess to it that was not unappealing. She knelt to take his forecock in her mouth.

He shouted with surprised pleasure. She took her time with him, sliding her lips up and down the shaft slowly, curling her tongue around the bulbous head. She ran her tongue down the underside of his forecock and back up the front of his aft. With one hand to steady her on the floor, she used the other to cup his balls, alternating between the two sets and lightly scratching her fingernails along the sensitive, responsive skin.

He was panting, thrusting into her mouth with short, sharp jerks. She leaned over to cup both of his cocks in her hands, remembering how much Tai'en liked the trick and realized that Pryt'en's scent was different, interestingly enough.

Meanwhile, Tai'en's fingers stroked her clit, probing into her ass or pussy in time with the thrusts of her own hips. When he began to fill her, he did so with excruciating slowness. She felt every inch of his blunt-tipped cocks as he pressed slowly into her holes. He held her hips to keep her from arching back to complete his entry, and she had no other outlet but to suck on the cocks in front of her. She wrapped her lips around the two sensitive heads, sliding her tongue along first one shaft, then the other, her strokes getting faster along with Pryt'en's pistoning hips. Tai'en, in contrast, thrust into her with slow, deep strokes, filling her, yet creating a need for more.

Pryt'en was going to come. She felt his mind go bright purple just before his shuddering release filled her mouth with come from his aft shaft, on which she'd been sucking. Yet his forecock remained stiff, and his release held an undercurrent of anticipation. She glanced up at him in amazement. "I didn't know," she murmured, wiping at her lips.

"It is most unusual and difficult, but very pleasurable to withhold one release while experiencing the other," Tai'en said.

"Can you do it?" she asked her mate.

Amusement evident in his voice, he replied, "For my lady's pleasure." He withdrew his aft cock from her pussy and bent over her, his bone spurs digging into her back. "Does this please you?" he asked.

"Oh, yes," she murmured. His thrusts drew his aft cock over her swollen and aching clit. Finally he increased his speed, slamming into her. She would have fallen on her face if it weren't for Pryt'en's steadying presence.

Pryt'en smiled down at her. "There is so much about you that fascinates." His fingers teased her nipples and the sensation drew a line of desire straight into her groin. She tightened, and with a growl, Tai'en filled her from behind. Her cunt, empty, begged to be filled.

Having two men pleasure her—with four cocks—was more than she could have ever imagined in her wildest, most hedonistic fantasies. As if they'd read those fantasies, her two lovers moved to sandwich her. Pryt'en moved around behind her and plunged his forecock into her rear entry and Tai'en, his eyes holding hers, filled her hungry pussy. They began a back-and-forth rhythm unlike anything she'd ever felt before—even in the communion when she'd felt the desires and needs of hundreds, the physical parts had all been Tai'en's alone. But having two lovers, each with his own rhythm and unique qualities sent her mind reeling. Their bodies pinned hers between them and two sets of ultra-sensitive bone spurs pressed into her flesh. She felt herself building, opening, stretching wide.

She was the devourer. Hunger raged through her. She couldn't get enough. Her body bucked, meeting the thrusts of her lovers back and forth with desperate force. Her lips tingled, her tongue ached, her body felt like it was rearranging itself. She needed to feel his flesh in her mouth. She pulled Tai'en down close to her and sank her teeth into the flesh of his neck. An answering bite from behind her caused her hands to spasm around Tai'en's neck.

White light burned her eyes as the pleasure built to fever pitch and she suddenly needed space. She flung her head back as the orgasm slammed into her, her entire body convulsing around the cocks filling her, completing her. A long scream forced its way out of her throat as her body jerked. Dimly, she heard a sharp cry from Tai'en, but it came from far away.

She felt them come, following her as she abandoned self and joined the universe.

Chapter Twelve

Instead of drifting lazily down from the heights of orgasm, she was jerked down and landed with a thud. Or more precisely, each of her lovers withdrew and Tai'en gathered her into his arms and set her down on a sleeping couch fast enough for her to wonder if she'd suddenly become contagious. The lavender hadn't even faded from their bodies, yet they were conversing urgently in Alcaini.

Swimming up from her lethargy, she tutted. "Was it that bad?"

Pryt'en held one of her arms and was studying it intently. Tai'en, meanwhile, put his thumb to her eyelid. She flinched.

"Please, 'iri, this is most unusual."

She let him poke his thumb in her eye. "If you must. But do you mind letting me in on exactly what's so unusual?"

"Do you not notice anything…different about yourself?"

Other than the suddenly ravenous sexual appetite and willingness to pursue it in ways heretofore unimaginable, not really. Her gaze traveled up her arm to the hand Pryt'en studied. It still held a hue of lavender peculiar to sexual afterglow but—*Oh.* "Oh," she repeated aloud, her lips going numb. She put two fingers in her mouth, and discovered to her immense relief that she still only had a plain old human tongue. "M-my eyes?"

Tai'en's lips folded into a grim line. "As Alcaini as the homeworld's moonrise."

Pryt'en dropped her hand. "It is best that we return to the mother vessel as soon as possible. The answers have a better chance to be found there." He settled himself in the pilot's seat.

Tai'en motioned to the harness above the sleeping couch. "Secure yourself. We will pilot the shuttle more swiftly than the gravity can react."

He strapped himself into the co-pilot's seat. Once she was harnessed herself, the craft shot forward with a burst of speed. The ride was bumpy, and speckled with frequent lapses in gravity where her nude body suddenly levitated itself off the sleeping couch and the only thing keeping her from being so much flotsam bouncing around the cabin was the harness. Docking maneuvers seemed interminable, and when the airlock finally hissed open, the three of them practically ran each other over trying to get out.

As they made their way to the medical bay, Rayne looked down at her body. Her skin had taken on a pinkish tinge that seemed to be deepening with each passing moment. Ez'iri met them at the medical bay's entrance. One look, and she nodded. "Come with me," she said to Rayne. When the men attempted to follow, Ez'iri's hand went up and stopped them. "This discussion is private."

Tai'en protested. "She is my mate. There are no secrets between us."

"I am her physician, kinsman, not you."

Anger darkened Tai'en's skin, but the color was washed out with an overlay of fear.

Ez'iri moved Rayne towards a smaller iris door. Even the bonds of matehood couldn't interfere with patient confidentiality, she guessed.

Once they were alone, Ez'iri wasted no time in debriefing her. "You are turning into an Alcaini," she said bluntly.

Rayne was oddly calm over the news. "I gathered. But how?"

"Irek'iri and I believe that the virus acted as some sort of agent."

Thank you once again, Kenneth. I hope your body's making some bottom-feeding fish very fat right now.

"The microbes injected into your body were designed to break down DNA. As the protein chains destabilized, the microbes could feed off the detritus and multiply. With nothing to brace your DNA, you would have disintegrated into a contagious corpse within two days. However, there existed the presence of something to replace the lost elements of your DNA, put there by your lover."

Her eyebrows went up. "You mean—Alcaini semen?"

"Precisely," Ez'iri said. "What you lost, Tai'en replaced, and actively eliminated what was breaking down your DNA."

"In other words," she said, the momentousness somewhat incomprehensible, "I mutated."

"Yes."

"And now I'm this hybrid Human-Alcaini mix."

"That is essentially correct."

She looked down at her arms, their skin tone deepening even further. With a look back up at Ez'iri, she said the only thing that jumped into her mind that even made half a lick of sense. "This is really going to clash with my hair color."

* ~ *

The fact that she was going native brought one thought to her mind that worried her more than anything else—if she turned Alcaini, would Tai'en still love her?

Romantic drama was shoved to the back of her mind once she entered Tai'en's quarters. He was preparing to leave again. "We are nearing homespace. Certain protocols must be observed," he said as he strapped on his armor plates.

The iris door swirled open a few minutes later. "The border patrols are hailing us," Pryt'en said tersely.

"They want us to quarantine all outworlders. Mother vessels from all over the system are being recalled." Pryt'en's hue was an ashen version of his normal ruddiness. She picked up on the tension, tensing even as Tai'en's features shaped themselves into a formidable frown.

Tai'en turned to her. "Return to the medical bay. You will be safest there."

"What's going on?" Nerves fluttered in her belly. The low, urgent tones held by the men made her fearful.

"We do not know. But homespace quarantine procedures are extremely stringent. And the recall of exploration vessels troubles me."

Almost as an afterthought, he tossed her a zap staff. "Take this."

She caught the staff and full-fledged dread came home to roost on her shoulders.

Before he left, he grabbed her and kissed her, hard. "You are mine," he said. "And I will keep you. Now go."

If she couldn't be with Tai'en, she could be with Ez'iri, and maybe get some answers. As she made her way to the medical bay, she passed groups of Alcaini on their way to other places. Many smiled at her, or reached out to touch her hair or her body. Others wore dark looks. All projected anxiety she could nearly taste. The medical bay was not the quiet refuge she'd hoped for.

Irek'iri was in a towering rage, her skin nearly black and her eyes flashing. She spit Alcaini invective in a shrill voice. Rayne caught one word in five, but the general gist of it was that Irek'iri was talking revolution. She looked to Ez'iri for translation.

Ez'iri's face was drawn. "The elders have discovered our Communion. They are furious. Our clan is to be punished. The conservatives have called for a retraction of all our exploratory ships and the expulsion of any outworlders on the homeworlds."

"They are killing us!" Irek'iri burst out. "They believe the influence of outworlders is polluting our minds, when it is their old and outmoded ideas that strangle us from within!"

Belis'iri, looking as worried as Ez'iri, tightened her lips. "There is nothing we can do about that right now. Let us instead study Rayne'iri while we all still have the chance. I am sure she wishes to learn more of her condition."

Irek'iri jutted her jaw out mutinously, but let her friends lead her to the computer bank. Rayne joined them, propping the zap staff into the corner. As she studied the data the Alcaini had collected on her over time, a theory began to form in her mind. It would require a lot more study, and a lot more testing, and a control group, and a ton of additional research, but it might mean the difference between survival and extinction for her new family.

She was busy comparing DNA samples, and so absorbed in the amazing chain of events that she didn't hear the door open, didn't hear Irek'iri's cry of protest, or Belis'iri's gasp. It was only when a heavy, unfamiliar hand thunked down on her shoulder did she realize something was amiss.

"Come with us, outworlder," a harsh voice said and she turned to see a squad of unfamiliar Alcaini, in full battle armor. Her zap staff stood useless in the far corner, and unlike Tai'en's clan, these Alcaini looked older and much less welcoming to outworlders.

When she met his eyes, the guard who had spoken gasped, but his grip didn't lessen. Irek'iri protested, stepping between her and the guard. This proved to be a mistake, as the guard shoved her aside and two of his associates held her immobile. A third jammed a zap staff up under her chin.

Sensitive to the hostility they radiated, Rayne rose slowly. She didn't think they'd appreciate it if she told them their animosity very poorly masked an unwilling fascination with her. "I will come," she said in Alcaini, hoping her accent didn't make her sound stupid.

Irek'iri's eyes filled with tears. "Rayne'iri," she said, "They will kill you."

Given the fact that she'd faced almost certain death numerous times in the past week, it was becoming a familiar companion. "They might as well take a number," she muttered, glaring at the assembled guard.

"The elders wish to speak to the outworlder before her execution," said the guard with the ham-like hand on her shoulder.

She rose slowly, and attempted to leave the room with a little of her dignity intact. Going hysterical wouldn't win her any points in the Alcaini mind.

They prodded her roughly, leading her to a part of the ship she'd never been to before—the bridge. A cluster of elder Alcaini gathered at the opposite wall of

the iris door. Their cranial bone spurs arched proudly
from their heads, some reaching nearly six inches in
height.

Tai'en, Pryt'en, and the rest of the clan's squadron
stood to one side of the elders, themselves surrounded
by guards. Something told her that, unlike Kenneth,
these guys knew how to use their zap staffs, and Tai'en
wouldn't get away with just being knocked out if they
decided to use them.

The elders approached her, but stopped several feet
away from her. One of them spoke to the assembled
room. "See this outworler, how she has caused the
greatest among you to betray his kind," he said in a
booming voice, pointing at Tai'en. "Mourn the loss of
the Alcaini children that could have been born to him
had he mated with a proper wife."

The guards and other elders bowed their heads,
emitting low, keening wails. The speaking elder looked
around with a satisfied smirk.

When the keening faded away, he looked around
again. "It is I who shall cut this cancer from our people.
The filthy practice known as Communion will not
happen when the outworlers do not exist to encourage
it."

Memories of the sense of oneness she experienced
at the Communion, and the joy and exultation
experienced by the Alcaini, multiplied and thrown back
at her a hundred-fold generated a cold anger in her.
How dare this single, bitter old coot attempt to befoul
something that had been incredible, and special, and

made so many happy all over his resentful personal opinions?

"Communion brings honor," she blurted out.

He rounded on her. "So the outworlder speaks our language? The outworlder understands? This outworlder, whose people are so numerous as to be a burden to their homeworld, dares to encourage a practice that causes more of our number to die childless every year?" He strode back and forth. "This outworlder is but an ignorant child, from an ignorant species, intent on killing itself and every other race they meet."

Come here and say that. "My people aren't the ones who ignore solid science just to preserve an outdated taboo!"

One of the soldiers whacked the zap staff against the backs of her knees. She went down hard.

"This outworlder," the elder continued, "makes farce of some of our most sacred beliefs. I will enjoy the honor of killing her for polluting our race *and* for her heretical disrespect of our culture."

Oh, blah, blah blah. She'd been hoping an elder might have sense enough to listen to her theory, and if she presented it eloquently enough, she might be able to turn a few heads and change a few minds. But the other elders were muttering among themselves, clearly distressed, but unwilling to fly in the face of their ringleader. *So that's how it is*, she thought grimly. She wouldn't change the leader's mind—he was too set in his hatred. But she might be able to sway the public's opinion. "It's my culture, too," she declared boldly. She rose to her feet and shrugged out of the grips of the soldiers holding her. In a flagrantly defiant motion, she flung her kimono from her shoulders, exposing her naked body. Behind her, she heard several of the soldiers gasp. She stood silent for a moment, allowing them the full view of her body, stoking their curiosity. She began to move slowly, speaking quietly. "Look at my skin. Look at my eyes. I have had Communion with Alcaini, and I am becoming Alcaini." She turned to the soldiers behind her, giving them a full frontal eyeful. "Have none of you ever wondered at the motivation behind your desire for outworlders?" She turned to face the elders. "Did it ever once occur to you that you seek us out for mates because *we become like you*?"

The elder was shocked. "Disgusting," he cried out, waving his zap staff. Behind her, she felt the soldiers begin to shift. As she looked around, she caught Tai'en's eyes. They glimmered with a tiny hope and gave her the courage to go all out. She bent over at the waist and put her fingers on either side of her labia, pulling her pussy lips apart. "I am like you," she said. "And yet I am different."

A sharp intake of breath behind her told her that her shocking behavior had an effect on at least one person. She brought her head back up. "Nothing in your history indicates that outworlders—or Communion— contributed to your race's decline in population."

"She speaks heresy!" The Elder shouted, his skin going darker and darker with each word. But she noticed the dark began to take on a purplish hue.

She played on that, cupping her breasts and lifting them. "See how my skin begins to change?" Bands of eggplant rippled beneath the elder's skin. Waves of revulsion rolled off him, but they were waves of self-revulsion.

"Denying your fascination with outworlders kills the Alcaini spirit as much as your infertility kills your race," she said, staring at the elders, willing them to listen to what she had to say.

The head elder had had enough. He flung his zap staff out and struck her hard on the shoulder.

She crumpled, pain shooting through her, hot on the heels of bitter disappointment. She almost had them!

Murmurs rippled through the crowd. She looked down at her chest. Her skin had yellowed with the sharp rush of pain from the blow. Over in the corner, a scuffle broke out as Tai'en struggled against the grips of his captors.

He wrenched free of them, suffering several forceful zap staff blows, but he made it over to where she knelt, his skin a shade of determined crimson. His eyes were full of pain as he went to help her stand.

As he gripped her arm, she was struck by a sudden flash of inspiration. Most of these soldiers weren't that old. They had probably never experienced a Communion. There had to be at least a little resentment over that. Instead of rising with him, she pulled him down.

Boldly, she slipped her hand beneath his loincloth and cupped him. "What..." he whispered.

But the lavender flush came quickly, as if it had been lurking there, just beneath the surface, waiting to be summoned. She pushed him down on his back and mounted him suddenly, swiftly, arching backwards to accommodate him.

No dim lighting presented shadows in which they could hide, no drums sounded to drown out the sense of—presence—that dozens of pairs of eyes glued to them produced. No chase built the tension or heightened the desires of hunter and prey. Yet she saw in his eyes what must surely be reflected in her own.

Anytime, anywhere, anyplace. Desire came when summoned. She ran her fingernails down Tai'en's chest and he hissed, capturing her hand in his as his hips began to move.

A gasp rippled through the room and the elder's eyes flashed with rage. "Cease!" he cried out "This abomination must stop!"

She closed her eyes, not to avoid the look of black fury on his skin, but to better sense how everybody else felt.

Curiosity about her radiated in the minds of all the soldiers around her. The urge to step forward and touch, to stroke her hair, massage the soft globes of her breasts, to taste her nipples with their forked tongues hit her from all sides.

She became aware of a low thumping in time with the pistoning of Tai'en's hips. The guards were striking the butt ends of their zap staffs on the floor in a heartbeat rhythm that reached into her chest and pulled her own heart into sync with it.

The elder moved forward, raising his zap staff. Rayne's eyes followed the arc of the staff as it came down sharply on her shoulder once, twice, then—

She felt, amidst the sexual energy, another, deeper thread of thought. These elders, they kept the mystery of Communion away from the young ones for so long, their words spewing terms like "abomination" and "sin," yet the tones of their voices thick and soft, belying the words.

Another staff blocked it. And another, and another, until they were encircled by the soldiers. She felt the elder's fury, self-loathing mingling with unwilling desire. With a mighty effort, she closed down that part of her mind that accepted that. Never again would she feel shame or loathing towards her desires.

Release came on the wings of sudden freedom. Love and sex and desire and the purposes of the universe mingled together and exploded as a supernova in the back of her brain, to the thrusting beat of Tai'en's cocks plunging in and out of her. As the stars faded from her vision, a soul-deep peace settled in their place.

* ~ *

Several hours later, she felt strong enough to leave the medical bay. Ez'iri had treated her bruises, which included a broken clavicle, with her crystals, and Irek'iri had told her what happened after the impromptu Communion.

"Abrus'en escaped us, taking half the elders with him." Scorn dripped from her voice when she mentioned the name of the Elder who'd been so violently opposed to her very existence. "That was a very brave thing you did. Had he taken an older squadron of guards, they might not have been so quick to rebel."

Tai'en found her later, staring out a viewport in one of the dining halls. Wordlessly, he slipped his arms around her. "Many of the elders still believe Abrus'en has the right of things."

"And the others?"

"May be willing to listen." His face, reflected in the viewport, held a mysterious smile. "Your boldness impressed them. But many minds must be changed. Our people have built a societal foundation on the preservation of our species."

She leaned back into him, taking comfort from the bone spurs that dug into the pressure points along her spine. "I've been thinking about that. Have your people ever kept long-term outworlder mates?"

"Not as single mates. Alcaini traditionally have taken other Alcaini first, then outworlders as their lifestyle allows. Except for me." His white teeth flashed in a grin, reflected from the dark viewport.

She looked down at her body. Beneath the short tunic she wore, her skin glowed with a ruddy sheen that surprisingly didn't clash as much with her hair as she'd originally suspected. She and Ez'iri had worked out a daily checklist to determine the rate of her change from human to Alcaini. So far, the skin tone and the eyes were the only physical signs of her transformation. She trailed her hands down the front of her tunic, feeling the tiny, firm knots between her breasts and at either side of her navel. Perhaps in a few weeks, she might sprout bone spurs, as well. While her case was unique because of the virus she'd carried, she suspected it wasn't unique in history—given enough time, she'd bet good money on long-term outworlder mates taking on more Alcaini physical properties. But she wasn't ready to advance that theory without the proper research.

She smiled to herself. There was still a little of the old clinical Rayne Warren in her. But there was someone new, too. Someone who found her heart's desires and kicked off the shame that others would insist she should feel. She rather liked this new person, and looked forward to getting to know her.

They stood silently, embraced, staring out at the endless stars for a long while.

Eventually, she turned. "What will happen to us, do you think?" she asked, looking up into his eyes.

"Until the balance of prevailing attitudes shifts again, the homeworld is closed to the clan." His arms tightened around her. "So we will go forward," he said. "Find others who will listen. And those who will not, we will try to change their minds." He placed his forehead against hers, a gesture so intimately tender it brought tears to her eyes. "I am sorry I was not able to bring you to my fine villa. I am sorry I have no gardens for your pleasure."

She put her hand on his cheek. "It doesn't matter," she said, meaning every word. An old cliché from Earth popped into her head. "Life's a journey, not a destination. Wherever we end up, at least we'll go there together."

THE END

About the Author:

Xandra Gregory writes ultra-hot erotic romances about extraordinary lovers in exotic settings. When she's not galaxy-hopping through the Civilized Worlds, she lives in the American Midwest, in the middle of a cornfield, which everyone knows is the best place for starships to land without getting harassed by the government.

Xandra writes for Liquid Silver Books and is an active member of Romance Writers of America, and the Passionate Ink Erotic Romance chapter.

www.xandragregory.com

The Best of LSB Romance...

The Zodiac Series
24 LSB Authors

12 books, a book a month from March 2005, each book featuring two stories about that month's Zodiac star sign.

http://zodiacromance.com

Ain't Your Mama's Bedtime Stories
Best Anthology of 2003 - The Romance Studio

R. A. Punzel Lets Down Her hair - Dee S. Knight
Beauty or the Bitch - Jasmine Haynes
Snow White and the Seven Dorks - Dakota Cassidy
Little Red, The Wolf, and The Hunter - Leigh Wyndfield
Once Upon a Princess - Rae Morgan
Petra and the Werewolf - Sydney Morgann
Peter's Touch - Vanessa Hart

Resolutions
4 ½ Stars Top Pick - Romantic Times BookClub

A Losing Proposition - Vanessa Hart
Free Fall - Jasmine Haynes
For Sale by Owner - Leigh Wyndfield
That Scottish Spring - Dee S. Knight

More Science Fiction Romances from LSB...

The Huntress
Barbara Karmazin

Sonia and Rulagh become The Huntress and Alien in Black. They create a team of aliens and humans and, in the process of working together, forge a love that transcends species.

At the Mercy of Her Pleasure
Kayelle Allen

NarrAy Jorlan hires thief Senth Antonello to steal an item for the Resistance. Their blossoming romance derails when her enemies kidnap his brother to get the item back. NarrAy's best option to save him could kill them all and plunge the entire empire into war.

Portal
Sydney Morgann

An erotic space romp that will have you holding your sides with laughter while panting for sexual release.

Liquid Silver Books

Quality Electronic and
Trade Paperback Books

http://www.liquidsilverbooks.com

Formats available:

HTML
PDF
MobiPocket
Microsoft LIT
Rocket eBook RB

Printed in the United States
95683LV00001B/14/A